The Gift Across the Street

By

K. Iwancio

Chapter One

"What the hell."

Grumbling more out loud and less under her breath than she meant, Clara's petite frame was having the darndest time trying to manhandle the Christmas tree off the roof of her smaller SUV. The lovely older gentleman at the quintessential picturesque tree farm had been able to help her but she neglected to figure out logistics for when she got home. At this point Clara was probably making a scene, spouting obscenities at her Christmas tree while hanging from the roof of her white car.

There was the clanking and rustling of what sounded like trash being put out. Clara grimaced at the thought of having an audience during her embarrassing wrestling match. A wrestling match that she was unfortunately losing. If worse comes to worst, she could just decorate the tree and leave it on her car. With a disgruntled brush of her dark blonde hair out of her gray-blue eyes, she attempted the feat once again.

Why the hell she thought that this year would be a good year to attempt to navigate the majesty of a live tree was beyond her at this point. This was Clara's first Christmas being hopelessly single and with no family close by. She was determined to make the most of it by starting new traditions and keeping up with her old favorites. This new tradition of a live Christmas Tree was one that she was quickly and wholeheartedly regretting.

Clara had, what she thought was, the clever idea of opening her car door and standing on the floor of her car to awkwardly bend around the roof to get closer to the incredibly tight knots that were just beyond her short reach. Wobbling a bit, she tried to adjust her grip on the twine. Between the mud from the farm and her rubber ankle boots, she lost her footing and unwillingly submitted herself to falling on her bottom to completely round out the ensemble.

What she wasn't expecting was a pair of strong arms and a torso to catch her. Her entire body startled.

"Whoa…easy there. You all right?"

Okay so maybe she did fall and hit her head and was lying unconscious on her driveway because she was fairly certain that she heard the words voiced in an impossibly polished and equally delectable English accent. Blinking, she tried to figure out if she was indeed all right.

"Oh um…I think- "

Clara had managed to regain some brain activity and her footing before turning around to her rescuer. Only to be rendered utterly speechless at the apparent state of him. He was incredibly handsome with a sharp jawline that dipped down to a dimpled chin. The eyes gazing down at her were full of concern and were the richest cerulean blue color that she had ever seen. Cropped auburn hair was an impossibly tousled crown upon his head. Although the tidbit that had ceased her breathing was the fact that he was very much shirtless and deliciously sculpted like a fine marble Renaissance statue.

"You think…?" he asked expectantly as he kept his arms to either side of her to make sure she wasn't going to pass out on him or anything.

"Oh…yes…I mean I'm fine." Clara managed to mumble out before a surprisingly sultry, "Thanks to you."

The chuckle was warm and made her body tingle, causing her brain to go off-kilter once again.

"Do you need help…?" The stranger asked with a nod of his head to gesture to the Christmas tree that had been her nemesis for the past thirty minutes.

Blushing, she averted her gaze with her sheepishness. "Is it that obvious?" Managing a breathy laugh, she shrugged. "I believe I overcommitted."

"Seems that way." Nodding with another chuckle he shoved his hand into his jogger pocket and procured a multi-tool of some kind. Her eyes were now drawn to the slim-cut joggers that left little to the imagination. Stepping up onto the floor of her car he effortlessly cut the ties and set her tree free in a matter of seconds.

"Do you…always keep weapons on you when wearing your pajamas?" Clara asked teasingly, feeling rather foolish about the fact that she had never bothered to run inside to grab scissors to make her current situation easier. Although had she done that then she wouldn't be in her driveway conversing with an incredibly handsome mystery neighbor.

"Only when I'm tidying my place. I fix things as I go." Stepping down he gathered the twine and handed it to her before stepping around her vehicle in his suede clog slippers. It was a peculiar mix of outfit but honestly, she had never seen anything sexier. "I was taking out the trash when I saw your…predicament." He spoke nonchalantly as if rescuing damsels in distress was a pastime.

"I wasn't swearing too loud, was I…?" she asked, rather embarrassed that she was causing a scene on the quiet street. Those eyes caught her off guard again as he peeked his head around the back end of her vehicle with an impossible grin.

"Maybe a little." He teased her and she felt her entire body run hot. Although she couldn't tell if it was from embarrassment or from the way he looked and spoke to her. Hefting the stump, he was already sliding the tree off the back end of her car roof and stood it up with ease. It was a rather short tree as she was afraid that she wouldn't be able to

5

properly decorate anything taller. Thankfully, the kind stranger was a few inches taller than her, and she was only a little jealous that he could put the star on with ease.

"Fucking shit, sorry." Clara flushed, realizing her error. "And I'm sorry for swearing again." All the handsome stranger could do was chuckle with a shrug.

"Nothing I haven't heard before. Although you may have given Mrs. Fitz a heart attack had she heard anything."

Gulping, she realized her error. The widow next door was an absolute treasure to Clara. She was just like the grandmother that unexpectedly passed the year before and whom she missed so extremely much. Either would have been mortified to hear her say one iota of even a questionable swear word.

"Oh well...good point." The neighbor was standing there in all his delicious glory, looking at her expectantly. With the color rising once again to her cheeks in her bashfulness with her next question. "Do you think you could help me bring it inside? You make it look so easy."

"I was going to offer...but I didn't want to invite myself in." His smile was soft as he dipped his chin with his dose of bashful politeness. Swallowing hard she bent to reach down to grab ahold of the stump, but he gestured with the jut of his chin for her to grab onto the top of the tree as he maneuvered over to the hefty stump.

"Uh...let me unlock and get the door first." With a quick nod, she turned on her booted heels and walked a few feet to her front door under her covered porch to unlock and push it open. Turning around, Clara just about ran into him as he had wordlessly hefted the tree onto her front step without much effort.

Noting her surprise, he shrugged with a grin. "I know you wanted to help but honestly it's not that bad to maneuver myself." The flex of the muscles in his biceps and chest was subtle as he picked up the tree again and stepped inside and past her open-mouthed expression. How was this gem of a being hiding across the street?

Regaining some measure of composure, she followed him inside and gestured to her bay window. Clara had already set the tree base there before she left to get her tree. When she had purchased her home earlier in the year in order to relocate for her job, all she had looked forward to was putting her Christmas tree in front of that window. She wanted to enjoy the glow of the lights with a fire going in the fireplace that's on the wall adjacent. As she was lost in thought, he had dropped the tree's stump into the base and flawlessly adjusted the tree and left it perfectly straight and level.

"Wow. My savior." Clara grinned, completely impressed and entirely thankful despite her subtle tease. There was a soft shade of pink that infiltrated his cheeks as he rose, brushing his hands off as if it was nothing.

"Plenty of experience." He stepped back over to her, his eyes subtly flitting about her face and rosy cheeks as if he was drinking it all in. Blinking, she shook her head, tossing the loose ponytail about. She was so desperately single that she was looking for any tiny hint of interest from an impossibly handsome stranger. "I've had a real tree every year since I could remember. There's something of a science to it. Glad I could help."

As much as Clara wanted to grab him and kiss him in her overwhelming thanks, she settled for putting her hand out for a handshake. "Well thank you. You did save me today."

Taking her hand with ease she felt wild electricity shoot up her arm from his touch. It only fanned the embers of fire from her first sight of the man when she was in his arms. There was a subtle flicker in his eye of some sort of surprise and she wondered if he felt that attraction too. By some miracle, she managed to utter her name along with her continued thanks.

"Clara."

"Nicolas. But I prefer Nic." He offered but kept his hand clasped with hers. The two of them zoned out for a long moment as she spent the time admiring and wallowing in the heat of his touch. Flexing her hands subtly she noted the stickiness of the residual sap and immediately scowled and felt terrible.

"Oh gosh, I didn't realize you were covered in sap! Do you want to wash your hands?" Her offer finally pulled the two of them apart but only with some minor trouble as the sap was fairly strong. They ended up in a fit of laughter as Nic nodded and followed her into the kitchen, admiring the place as he went. She let him go ahead and handed the grease-cutting dish soap to him. "This works better than the hand soap."

Clara watched him wash his hands, taking care to get the stickiness of the sap off as best he could. He was methodical in his cleansing. She took a moment to appreciate that as he had no issue hanging out with a strange neighbor that he had just met. Finally satisfied, he dried his hands on the hand towel hanging on her oven door before giving her the space to wash her own hands.

It was quick work as he only had given her some residual sap transfer and she continued to chuckle over what was transpiring. Walking back into the living room, Nic was busying himself with removing the netting from around the tree with his handy pocket knife. Clara stood there, completely in awe that this man was going above and beyond to help her. Her last few boyfriends would never have taken this kind of initiative without her asking first.

"Sorry, I just figured while I was here…and with the right tools, that I'd help you out." Noting her staring, he shrugged sheepishly as he gingerly pulled the rest of the netting off and let the tree fluff out to a satisfying plumpness. Stepping over to him she took the netting to dispose of without hesitation. It was just utterly delightful to stand that close to him again.

"Seriously, you're the best thing ever." The words spilled from her mouth quickly before her brain could even register what her body was shouting. A flush to her cheeks was immediate as she both reveled and regretted her words in the same instance. Dipping his chin, he used the motion to hide his demure look.

"Just glad I could help a damsel in distress." If only Nic had been able to hear her internal awkwardly desperate wilting whimper, he would have run straight for the hills. "Although, I should get back. I wanted to finish tidying the rest of the place up and relax a bit before work tomorrow. It was nice to meet you."

Unable to say much else, she nodded with a crooked smile. "Oh shit, it's freezing out there." The words tumbled out in a heap as she was pulling the plaid wool throw from the back of the chair closest to her. "Seriously, take it. You'll make me freeze just watching you step outside." With a laugh, he glanced out Clara's window as the snow had started to fall while the two of them were messing with her tree.

Leaning in with a nod and a deliciously warm chuckle Nic took her offering without hesitation. Wrapping it around himself like a shawl, he grinned and cast a glance at her. "Thank you. I could probably manage to survive the short distance, but I'll appreciate the warmth. See you around." There was a slight tip of the fingers to salute her as he opened the door with one last look at Clara.

Scrambling to hide behind her tree, Clara watched him saunter across the street. His hands adjusted the throw to tightly encompass him against the obscenely large fluffy flakes and subtle chilly breeze. She wanted to see what apartment he went into so that perhaps she could stalk/stop by. Clara had to retrieve her throw one day, right? Although with all the help he offered today her entire being wanted to invite him over for dinner to say a proper thank you.

If only she could figure out how to muster up the courage.

Chapter Two

The work week rolled around, and Clara had barely managed to pull herself from her warm bed to get up for the drudgery of work. Especially when most of the nights she was lost in those imagined strong arms of the neighbor across the street. Nic had been impossibly kind, maybe even borderline flirtatious and her mind couldn't stop reeling from the chain of events. She may have spent the last few days trying to keep an eye on his place to note his schedule, but the man hadn't left his apartment since the weekend.

Sipping her coffee, she stepped into the living room into the bright light of day. There was a decent coating of snow still on the ground from the storm Sunday afternoon and it made the sheltered light of the sun more brilliant despite the early hour. All Clara had managed to do after Nic left was get some lights on the tree before she needed a cold shower and some…personal time before bed. She honestly couldn't remember the last time that she had been that hot and bothered by the mere presence of the opposite sex in the same room.

The view out the window behind her lit tree struck her suddenly and she had the greatest urge to bake Christmas cookies. Wandering over to her work laptop, still open on her kitchen island from her after-hours work session the night before, she clicked through her calendar for the rest of the day. Clara noted the lack of meetings and appointments for the afternoon, a welcomed reprieve for the mid-week.

Promising herself an afternoon off, she set off for the office, making a mental shopping list for her cookie endeavor.

The workload was steady, even despite her working ahead the last few nights. The few hours until noon passed fairly quickly. During downtime between emails, she decidedly settled on sugar, gingerbread, and peanut butter blossom cookies. Simple and traditional recipes that were handed down to her by her beloved late grandmother. Clara's mouth was already watering from the thought of taste-testing later.

The grocery store was on the way home and she stopped to gather her ingredients. Perhaps something also for lunch as the thought of the leftovers in her fridge sounded less than appealing. First, she had to accomplish the scavenger hunt down the baking aisle. Currently, the natural vanilla extract was eluding her.

"Clara?"

The utterance of her name in the form of a question stalled her efforts and she furrowed her brow in confusion for a moment as she turned toward the voice. She could have sworn it sounded like…

"Nic." She breathed out in surprised disbelief as the two of them stood arm's length from each other in the aisle.

"Hi." His smile was beautifully warm and inviting and he looked genuinely pleased to run into her. "Looking for something in particular?" Blue eyes drifted to the shelf behind her. Keeping this little tidbit to himself, he had been watching Clara for the longest time, enticingly bent over in her search for the extract. The cut of her pencil skirt that she had worn to work hugged her curves just right. He had to swallow down the heat before gathering the courage to say something.

"Oh." Blinking through her mind fog at his sudden reappearance in her life, she was still stuck on the soothing cadence of his accent. "Well yes. Trying to find the natural vanilla extract." Flushing, she did her best to ignore the fact that here he was, coming to her rescue yet again.

With a quick furrow of his brow, Nic must have mustered some x-ray vision magic and easily swooped down to pull a bottle off the shelf. "You mean this?" His grin was teasing. Clara swallowed at the closer positioning of his body to hers.

"I'm not normally this helpless, I swear." She offered quickly with a minor nervous tremor in her voice as she took the bottle from him and put it in the shopping basket on her arm. The jest had him erupting with laughter and he flashed her another smile.

"It's all right, I don't mind. Gives me more of an excuse to run into you." The curl that hit her lips was simultaneous with the implosion currently going on in her body. "You never know when one might need saving."

Oh, the things Clara wanted to say and do to that man in the grocery store, at that very moment, would have made even a porn star blush. "Well…consider me lucky that you're my knight in shining armor this week." There was a tinge of pink to the apples of his cheeks, surrounding that delightful beauty mark on his right cheekbone.

Adjusting his stance somewhat uncomfortably, he cleared his throat and managed to elude the jumble of sultry thoughts wreaking havoc in his brain. "So…um…what are you baking?"

"Oh…uh Christmas cookies. I love making them every year from scratch."

"Oh my, that sounds delightful. What kind do you like to make?"

"Well, I'm planning on sugar, gingerbread, and peanut butter blossoms."

"Damn…it's been some time since I had a decent sugar cookie." He mused thoughtfully. The basket of items that Clara had already acquired was digging into the crook of her arm. She adjusted her stance to hold it with both of her arms in front of her. The pressing together of her biceps gave a plump uplift to her breasts and her cleavage became much more easily visible from the neckline of her blouse. His eyes flickered down and hovered for longer than he meant. "Ah well…I'd better get going. My lunch break goes by too quickly to get much shopping done. Maybe I'll run into you again?"

Clara said her farewell before turning and watching Nic head down the rest of the aisle. He disappeared around the corner before she could manage to breathe. In her desperation, she was hopeful that maybe he felt some semblance of the chemistry that she felt radiating off of him. As for right now, she had a new mission. To make the best damn sugar cookies for that cookie across the street.

Chapter Three

Clara's afternoon had been spent blasting Christmas rock music as she whipped up three dozen of each flavor of cookie. The sugar cookies had been first as she wanted them to adequately cool before decorating them. Plopping down onto a stool at her island she mixed up the simple ingredients to make the icing glaze for the sugar cookie snowflakes. The mindless activity allowed her mind to wander as she drew the simple lines, piped with care from the icing bag.

It was in those long moments, where Clara was piping the second dozen, that she had a eureka moment. She was already set on making Nic's sugar cookies, but she still had to deliver them. Why not deliver them with an invitation to dinner? Her typical straight icing lines wavered a bit with the nervousness from her thought. The worst he could say was no, right? But the absolute best was if he said yes. She just needed to shoot her shot. What else was she going to do on a Friday night except perhaps dive into a carton of ice cream to go with her cookies and binge Christmas movies? She would need some help getting the star on the tree anyway…

Pulling out an appropriately sized plastic container Clara carefully placed a mix of a dozen sugar cookies and half a dozen each of the gingerbread and peanut butter blossoms. Glancing at the time it was just after 7 pm and that was hopefully a more than acceptable time to knock on his door with her offering and invite. Her nervousness started to outweigh her clever idea, but she had to kick it and stuff it out the window. She needed to see that wildly attractive man across the street again and give him an excuse to (hopefully) see her again.

Adjusting her coat, Clara swallowed down what was the last bit of apprehension before she coaxed herself to knock on his door. There was some rustling. Her heart began to beat impossibly fast as she heard the lock being undone before his hand moved to the handle. She immediately felt the warmth of his apartment against the chill outside, but his smile warmed her from the inside out.

"Someone told me that you had a craving for some good sugar cookies." Clara managed to utter in a remotely suave manner as she presented the container of cookies. Blue eyes stayed on her face for a long moment before he addressed the gift with a delighted chuckle.

"I'm glad you understood the subtlety of my hint." Grinning, he took the container into his hands with a sparkle of satisfaction. There was a long moment of silence as he shifted, stuck in some kind of internal argument.

Clara made the motion to leave, and his sudden response startled her slightly. "Do you want to come in for some tea or cocoa?" That enticing heat blossomed across her skin under her camel-colored coat and the chilly air outside suddenly grew insufferable. She mulled over the invitation for a second, reminding herself of the disaster of a kitchen back home that still needed to be cleaned.

Fuck it.

"Oh... I'd love to." Smiling softly, she turned back to his door. He stepped aside with a gesture of his hand, still holding the container of cookies. The apartment was small but rather quaint and cozy. He had some sort of makeshift office across his coffee table and his work had spilled onto the rest of the sofa, radiating out from the end seat.

"Sorry...the chaos of a work deadline and the surprise of a cookie delivery do not mix well for company." He chuckled nervously and tried to usher Clara quickly into the much neater kitchen, save for a few dirty dishes in the sink.

"Nothing that I haven't seen before. I've had that kind of week myself." She reassured him as she sank into one of the wooden chairs surrounding his round kitchen table. Placing the container on the table he quickly busied himself with gathering mugs and filling up his electric kettle before setting it to boil.

"So, what do you do for a living?" Nic asked as he pulled down his container of tea. She was eyeing his impressive selection from over his shoulder. "Did you want tea or cocoa?"

"Tea, please." Clara couldn't help but notice that satisfied little smile to himself, finding delight in her choice. "Oh, and I'm a graphic designer for a marketing company. Nothing but deadlines." The words were flowing with ease now that there was a table between the two of them, all the while ignoring the fact that she was now in his apartment. "What about you?"

"Senior research consultant for a tech giant. Unfortunately, I can't say much more than that." He chuckled and she pursed her lips with intrigue.

"Oh no that's fine, I doubt I could figure out anything beyond that even if you were able to explain it." Clara joked as he placed the tea organizer on the table in front of her before tending to the whistling kettle. He filled two mugs with ease and wandered back over.

Comfortable clothes seemed to be his staple and she was thankful that he worked from home and wasn't some loaf. He was still wearing his skinny jeans from the earlier encounter at the grocery store. What had her intrigued now was the navy V-neck t-shirt that seemed to be one size too small. Even fully dressed she could easily make out the shape of his muscles from their first interaction.

Settling into his chair, Nic was eyeing the container of cookies as he slid her mug over. Only at that moment did Clara ever wish to be a plastic storage container to be on the receiving end of a hungry and desperate look from such an attractive man.

Clearing her throat, she started thumbing through the tea as he opened the lid of the cookie container and took a moment to breathe in the encased aroma. "I hope they live up to your expectations." she said rather sheepishly as she busied herself with making her cup of tea.

"Considering how lovely they look; I'll be quite pleased if they even taste half as good." Dipping a hand in, he grabbed a sugar cookie off the top and immediately brought it to his mouth, leaving his hot water mug completely forgotten. The guttural groan he made went directly between Clara's thighs and her flush was wildly hot behind her mug as she carefully sipped its contents. If her baking managed to bring out those kinds of noises from him, she was more than eager to see what she could do with her body. "These are fucking amazing."

Laughing away her fluster, she cast him a long and adoring look. He was so lost in some kind of euphoria, and she drank it in, filing that sight away for bedtime later. "I'm glad you like them." He shoved the rest of the cookie into his mouth without further question and his cheeks protruded slightly with the awkward size of the remainder. He chewed slowly for a moment before turning to his tea. "Seriously, these are really good." His mouth was still full, and he chewed the last bit quickly in his embarrassment before swallowing. "Thank you."

"Well...I wanted to say thank you for helping me this weekend. Coming to my rescue before I made a total ass of myself."

"Glad I was in the right place at the right time to assist." Shifting in her seat, Clara was trying to muster up the courage once again to invite the man to dinner before he orgasms over her cookies alone. It gave her some semblance of hope for even a chance with him later. "So...do you do anything else besides bake and work?" Nic seemed eager to continue their casual conversation and she lost her nerve to ask her question.

"Well…I suppose I'm creative outside of work. I like to paint with watercolors and acrylics." Shrugging, Clara downed the rest of her tea. He had quite a delectable selection and she was eager for another cup. Quick to her aid, and with another mouthful of cookie he refilled her cup. "And travel. But since I bought the house, I haven't been able to do much of that lately."

"I love to travel too. My excuse is the workload. Even if I could take time off there would be four times as much to do when I got back." Clara nodded and laughed softly in her agreement as she made her second cup of tea.

"There is always that. I try not to look at my emails while I'm away but coming back to 300 or more is just…insane to deal with." Clara's eyes watched him from around the top rim of her mug as he devoured another cookie. "I think I'm going to have to make you more cookies." The tease was light, as he side-eyed her and looked rather sheepish as he munched on his fifth cookie.

"They're too delicious." Taking a sip from his lukewarm mug, he washed down the sweet crumbles. "I can't remember the last time I had such amazing baked goods."

Clara flushed with the compliment and couldn't help the tender little smile at the corner of her mouth. Step one was completed and completed with the utmost satisfaction. Now she just needed a clever segway and the nerve to ask him over. "I hope I didn't spoil your dinner…"

Laughing heartily, he grinned at her and only looked a little bit guilty. "Technically…but I'm considering this an appetizer." Reaching for the kettle, he poured a bit more of the hot water into his mug to warm up what was left of his now cold tea.

"Oh well…um…speaking of dinner…" Clara started uneasily, trying to find a suitable cadence to her words. Thankfully he was still quite absorbed in his tea and cookies. "I was wondering…" The softer tone of her words had enticed his eyes over to hers in what looked like delighted expectancy. With his full gaze on her, her nerve was quickly running in the opposite direction. Squinting, her eyes closed, she just decided to let him have it. "I was wondering if you'd like to come over for dinner on Friday."

Nic's eyes widened slightly in his muted excitement. The look he gave her was odd and she was beginning to freak out. Was he delighted with her request or completely mortified? She needed to cover herself. Just in case.

"To say thank you! I...I...wanted to thank you for your help on Sunday." His eyes immediately went to the container of cookies as he thought that was the thank you. Now he was thoroughly confused. "The cookies were just an appetizer." She said with a wry grin, teasing him right back. That drew a hearty bit of laughter from him.

"Fair enough." Nic shrugged and looked up at her with an earnest smile. "I'm free on Friday." Shrieking inwardly with her delight, she hoped he didn't notice her leg hopping beneath the table with her excitement. Until her knee nudged his. Clara's breathing immediately hitched, still locked halfway between her lungs and nose. He made no sudden movement and she hoped he didn't feel the touch.

In fact, Nic had felt her nudge his knee. He was currently biting the rim of the mug in a vain effort to stifle the rise of heat stemming from her innocent touch. To be honest with himself, he had been anxious to run into Clara since she moved into the neighborhood earlier that year. He had been looking for any lame excuse to talk to her and the fact that she needed help with her tree was the opening that he had been waiting for.

Now Clara was here, in his apartment, and as attractive and charming as he thought she would be. It was taking everything he had to not clear off his kitchen table and toss her on top of it. No woman has ever complimented him quite like she did. He had come to her rescue, on more than one occasion. That was a wild stroke to his ego to help out a lovely woman in her hour of need. To top it all off, the outrageously delicious handmade cookies were the icing on the rather erotic cake she had unknowingly constructed.

19

The clearing of her throat was a bit vigorous, and Clara downed the rest of her tea before rising up.

"Um...would six be good?" Nic rose only a half second after her, hoping that she wasn't leaving so quickly. Reaching for her coat, his face dropped a bit in her haste. Honestly, she wasn't sure if she could behave herself if she stayed even a moment longer.

"Uh...oh yeah. That would be great." Exasperated hands ran through his messy, cropped hair as he followed her forlornly to his door. Holding the door open for her he watched Clara pause and turn back around to him with a slow smile. There was still a tinge of hesitation as she really wanted to pull him in for a kiss. Considering that he was still technically almost a stranger, she kept her distance.

"See you Friday. I can't wait. Thanks for the tea." Her words came out in a rush, and she scampered down the steps, leaving Nic to watch her tiptoe with graceful care across the wet street to her front door. Maybe by Friday, he could wrack up the nerve to do more than talk to her.

Chapter Four

On Friday, Clara spent the day working from home so that she could clean her house to her utmost satisfaction. The outside of her home finally had the finishing touches of simplistic decorations. A handmade wreath on the front door and a garland across her porch with a spotlight to highlight it all. It complemented her historic Tudor cottage just perfectly. The bay window framed the twinkling white lights of her tree so well that someone could have pulled the scene out of a storybook.

The retrieval of her indoor Christmas decor and ornaments had been more of a hassle as she had amassed quite a collection. She was desperately hoping that she could convince her knight to assist with the tree decorating. More specifically the star on the tree. It was a beautiful Capiz shell Moravian star that lit up and was a bit fragile. She had high hopes for a flawless casual dinner, a Christmas movie, tree decorating, and probably the consumption of more cookies (among other things). Nic seemed like a good sport, but it may be wishful thinking to get all that on a first date.

Er…was it a date? It technically had all the earmarks of a date. Although Clara had pressed that it was a 'thank you' more than anything. Would he think it's a date? She would be completely okay with that. The thought stayed with her as she settled in to cook dinner. Something simple would be best as she was a much better baker than a chef. She wasn't terrible, as all the food she made was edible. Just nothing fancy.

Clara had settled on beef stew as it was easy to chop everything up and throw it in the slow cooker to bubble away all afternoon. Of course, she couldn't deny the baker in her and made an entire batch of baked-from-scratch biscuits to accompany their meal. Dessert was also on the menu, and she whipped up some caramel shortbread crumble bars. Her house felt warm and cozy and smelled divine. Add that in with the lights on the tree and with the fireplace going, and it was borderline magical. A regular damn Hallmark movie set if she ever subjected herself to one. All she needed was the hunky love interest and the ensuing romance. The love interest she had, the ensuing romance…remained to be seen.

Which reminded her, Clara needed to get herself ready with only thirty minutes to spare. After fretting all morning, she had settled on a lovely traditional red Stewart tartan blouse with black skinny jeans and her favorite fashionable slippers. Makeup was subtle since she planned to keep the lights somewhat low all evening to enjoy the Christmas tree instead. Her hair was half-pinned back for something that was effortlessly elegant and useful to keep the strands out of her face.

Glancing at the clock, there was just enough time to set the coffee table with the impromptu picnic. Having dinner in her living room was much less formal than in the dining room or kitchen table. Clara set out a bowl full of the biscuits, hoping that Nic would find them enticing, at least if her stew was subpar. Based on the smell it was going to be decent. Spoons and napkins came next. The last thing she managed to put out before the doorbell rang was wine glasses and drinking glasses, just in case. She didn't want to presume his choice of drink.

Clara's heart leaped to her throat, and she quickly turned on some holiday music. Giving herself a once-over in her foyer mirror and a quick brush of her palms down her blouse, she opened the door. The sight before her made her simultaneously combust and melt. The look on Nic's sweet face was some mix of excitement and delight that he was trying to smooth out and be cool about. The flannel he had on was rather festive in a subtle hunter-green and burgundy plaid. It was slim cut and perfectly suited for his lean body. He had a bottle fisted in his right hand, which hovered in midair for a moment, as the two of them just took each other in.

Fingers ruffled through his tousled auburn hair absentmindedly as he finally offered Clara the bottle of red wine. "Um…hi." He murmured somewhat bashfully. "I hope you don't mind I brought wine."

Cradling the bottle into her hands, she was reluctant to break his intense cerulean gaze, but she had to beckon him inside. "Hey." Clara smiled back as he stepped past and into her foyer, his eyes immediately drawn to the moody living room. "Actually, this red wine will go great with dinner." Glancing over his shoulder at Clara, she could see his shoulder sag in some relief.

"Oh, well…perfect then." Nic stood in her living room, slightly unsure of where he should go next. Noting his apprehension, she gestured to the sofa, all set up in front of the coffee table and the television that was playing popular Christmas music through the speakers.

"Have a seat on the couch." Clara offered as she put the wine on the table with the simplistic place settings and he quickly got the idea. Sitting down with ease, his gaze was already eying the bowl of biscuits and she chuckled to herself. "Are you hungry now? I can serve dinner."

"I see you're as classy as me, dinner on the sofa." His chuckle was warm and sweet. Nic was thankful for the casualness of the evening as he was rather unsure where she stood in her feelings towards him. The dim lights, fire, and candlelight had him leaning in a more romantic direction, but he didn't want to presume. "Dinner now sounds great. It smells amazing."

Laughing Clara blushed, unsure if she should be delighted or embarrassed at the setup. "Oh…well thank you. I hope you don't mind beef stew and biscuits. I figured it was fitting for a cold winter night." She excused herself with a shrug as he reached out to grab a biscuit. She could feel her heart warming as she dashed into the kitchen to fill bowls up for the two of them and grab her corkscrew.

Nic was already well onto his second biscuit and looked rather pleased with the outcome of her baking endeavor. "I think you have me hooked on your baking." He uttered around the bite of biscuit he had just taken before she reentered the room. Laughing, she placed his bowl in front of him on the coffee table before sitting down somewhat close. It wasn't right up against him, but it wasn't on the complete opposite side of the sofa either.

Grabbing the wine bottle, Clara managed to manhandle the cork with a resounding pop as he finished off his biscuit. She couldn't help but notice as he closed his eyes in complete enjoyment before eyeing up the steaming bowl of beef stew that she had placed on the table. Being the ever-polite gentleman and guest, he waited for her to pour the wine and settle in before grabbing his glass.

"To new memories and friends this Christmas." His grin was spirited, and he at least was respectful enough not to mention her embarrassing debacle back on Sunday.

"Here. Here," Clara added in hearty agreement with a flush to her cheeks and clinked her wine glass with his before tipping it back to sip at the contents. The wine was smooth and warming and she noted not to drink too much lest she lose control of her tongue and some of those feelings she kept buried. The two of them placed their glasses back down on the table before digging into the stew.

It was delightfully perfect, warm, and savory with satisfying chunks of veggies and beef. Clara breathed out a sigh of relief. So far, the evening was progressing without a hitch.

"Wow, this is fantastic," Nic mumbled through another large bite, and she giggled softly. "Definitely hitting the spot."

Clara reached out to grab a biscuit and took a thoughtful bite. "I figured it was easy for a snowy evening."

He nodded vigorously as he continued to enjoy his stew. She tried, as subtly as she could, to watch his reactions as he ate, which were just endearing and sweet. As much as he was enjoying his meal, she wanted to keep the conversation flowing.

"I am so glad the work week is done and over. Usually, it's not so busy with the holidays coming up. But this year...this year has just been insane."

Chuckling, he grabbed his napkin to wipe his freshly shaven face. "Agreed. What the hell is up with that? I'm hoping those emails die off until after the new year."

"Wishful thinking at its finest!" Clara laughed and took a long drawl of her wine before turning back to her bowl. Between the alcohol and a satisfying meal, her body was in full relaxation mode, and she tucked her legs up and under herself. "Any plans this weekend? Or are you just going to veg out, like I'm planning on?"

"Relaxing? Absolutely. But I was debating on going to the Christmas tree lighting in the square on Sunday evening. I try to go every year. Helps me get into the spirit a bit more."

"Oh, that sounds rather lovely. I can't say that I've ever gone to one of those."

"It's fun. They have a bunch of vendors and restaurants that are set up in either tents or little sheds so there's plenty to eat and try out. Plus, they flood one of the soccer fields in the park and set up an ice rink. You should go check it out." Nic was trying a hard sell on the event but was too apprehensive to outright ask her. Clara intimated him slightly. Even as a distressed damsel she was confident and effortlessly lovely.

Taking a long sip of her wine glass, she mustered up the courage to ask her next question. "Okay...so I know I asked you over to thank you for coming to my rescue on Sunday. But...I had an ulterior motive." She had risen from the sofa so quickly that she didn't notice the red-hot flush that had enveloped Nic's rather excited face. Was she going to admit she had feelings for him? Maybe offer to completely ravish him on the sofa?

"I also need help putting the star on my tree." Clara waved the star sheepishly from her position by the tree. Rapidly he swallowed down his sultry excitement and turned to look at her with one of his devastatingly handsome smiles. "You are my knight in shining armor after all," she added coquettishly with a smile, hoping that would stroke his ego. Although she had completely overlooked her unknown innuendo.

"Ah well…" He started as he rose from the couch to come and assist her without any hesitation. "How could I deny a lovely damsel?" Taking the star gingerly into his hands, he quickly set to work clipping it onto the vertical top branch with ease. She had to immediately dip her chin away from his as there was a violent blooming flush that rose to her cheeks as she bit her lower lip. Did he just compliment her? Or was he just playing her little teasing game?

In a matter of moments, he had the star plugged in and the additional light set a brighter glow to the subdued room. His blue eyes stayed on the majesty for a long moment as Clara moved her eyes up to survey his work. "Absolutely flawless. Thank you." Moving his hands to his hips he turned his gaze back to her with a shy smile. His eyes didn't stay long as they were now distracted by the various plastic ornament containers that she had on the floor around the tree.

"Glad I could assist. Do you…want help decorating your tree? I have to say it's my favorite kind of decorating to do…"

Her laughter was a soft putter with a tinge of delighted surprise. "That would be wonderful." With the music crooning in the background, the two of them set to work. Her containers were filled with an entire treasure trove of childhood memories. Explaining the ornament exchange tradition to Nic, gave him fuel to delve into her past. Her parents and relatives had gifted her with an ornament every year since she was born. Some were fun and some were given based on a life event or interest she had that year.

The rest of the evening was spent sharing stories of the past, the good and the bad, and the downright embarrassing. There were lots of smiles and laughter but most of all Clara was enjoying this close activity as the two of them brushed hands or arms more than once. She was becoming quite addicted to the flash of heat whenever they touched each other, knowingly or unknowingly. Discretely she tried to steal glances at him from the opposite side of the tree but more than once their eyes met with a shy flitting away.

Since her tree was small, the task didn't take very long. The two of them tried to muster all of their organizational and decorating tactics to get the tree completely covered in ornaments. Standing back to admire the work, Clara glanced over at Nic with a delighted smile. "I think our efforts deserve dessert."

He had crossed his arms as he stood back to look over the teamwork but uncrossed them in delight at the thought of one of her desserts. Trying to be additionally helpful, he gathered up the dirty bowls and utensils after topping off the rest of the wine bottle in each of the glasses. She heard him step into the kitchen as she was cutting up the caramel crumb bars and pacing them carefully into a shallow bowl. Glancing over her shoulder she caught him in mid-admiration of her. Or was it mid-drool over the dessert she was plating?

"Oh, thank you," Clara said softly in her appreciation as she moved on to scooping vanilla ice cream into each of the bowls. "You can just put them in the sink." He did so without question and with a smile before dipping back into the living room. Noting that the coast was clear, she halved out the beef stew and remaining biscuits and put them into two separate containers for him to take home. No sense in not letting him enjoy another helping or two later. Besides, there were enough there to feed her for a week.

Delivering the delectable dessert, Clara got a heartily approving noise of delight that made her squirm a bit against the couch cushions. How long is the appropriate amount of time to wait before one could violate a handsome neighbor in their home? Instead, she distracted herself by asking him innocent questions like what his favorite holiday movie was and his favorite Christmas carol. The ice cream was a welcomed reprieve from the heat simmering between when they had decorated the tree.

Finished with her bowl, Clara sat it down on the table with a muted clunk and leaned back into the cushions. She was close to him, but not too close, although there was more of the sofa available than what the two of them took up. Her eyes moved back up to the television screen and she watched it for a few moments before feeling a warm blush rise to her cheeks with that unmistakable feeling of being observed. Nic had finished the scrumptious desert long before she had devoured hers. Now he was completely entranced with her and the way that the glow from the television screen made her gray-blue eyes sparkle.

Clara's eyes shifted first before she tipped her chin over towards him. He stiffened slightly, realizing that he had been found out with his subtle admiration. The draw between them was strong and she felt herself leaning in ever so slightly with him mirroring her movements. It was too soon for this sort of thing, and she felt her mind protest for some unsightly reason. With a sharp hitch of her breath, she pulled away quickly. She rose up and gathered the empty dessert bowls with a quick smile.

"Uh…would you like more?"

Nic had to catch his breath before he could manage to answer. "As much as I'd love to say yes, I don't think I could possibly have another bite. My compliments to the chef…and baker. But actually…" He glanced at his watch and hesitated for the longest moment. Nic wanted nothing more than to stay longer but the early obligation the next day thwarted his efforts. "I should head out. I have to be at the men's shelter by 7 am to help with breakfast."

Clara couldn't help but feel a little disappointed behind being impressed at his fortitude. "Oh well...a noble deed for a noble knight. I couldn't hold you up from that."

Chuckling, he shoved his hands into his pockets in a vain effort to restrain himself. "Maybe I'll see you Sunday at the tree lighting? Thanks for dinner. You can have me over anytime." The grin he flashed her was a front for his joke, but he was honest about the latter part. He wouldn't mind any invitation at any time for any reason to her place.

"Oh! Before you go..." Clara dipped back into the kitchen quickly to put the bowls in the sink. He felt his body tense in morbid anticipation once again, hoping for a kiss or a hug...or something... Although he was more than elated when she quickly returned with two large plastic containers full of leftover stew and biscuits. Her heart warmed as his eyes widened in grateful delight. "You're set for dinner this weekend too."

"Wow. This is so great." He gratefully took the containers over into his possession with the tip of his head. "Thank you. They will be enjoyed very much." Now that her hands were free, she stepped over to her front door and opened it for him. He followed, pausing before her, giving her a warm smile as he walked out into the night. "Goodnight, Clara."

"Goodnight, Nic."

Chapter Five

Clara had spent the last two days debating showing up to the town's tree-lighting celebration. Big crowds really weren't her thing. Although Nic had made it sound like he was really hoping she would attend. Why he didn't just outright ask her in the first place was beyond her. She was stuck in a constant tumble of questions and replays of all their interactions. The two of them could talk about things so effortlessly and there was a relaxed comfort around him. As long as he wasn't slipping her those sultry kinds of glances or questionable flirts.

Making it just in time for the countdown of the lights and the start of the festivities. Clara found a spot away from the thick of the people and had a lovely view of the entire tree. Suddenly, the tree exploded in a fierce glittering twinkle of lights, and it was quite a sight to see. She was glad that she arrived when she did.

"Hello there." A puff of hot hair escaped her mouth, and the condensation of her breath encircled her head as she turned with a start. "I'm glad you made it."

"Nic!" She managed to breathe out as she looked him over, bundled in a navy peacoat and plaid woolen scarf. "...Hi." A smile crossed her lips as she was quite happy to see him. He would never mention it to her face, but he had been waiting on the outskirts of the park on a bench for her to arrive.

"Hot chocolate?" Lifting a brightly colored lidded cup he offered her one of the two in his hands.

"Oh, that's so nice of you, thank you." The walk to the town square had been cold, but she didn't want to bother with parking. Taking the cup into her hands, Clara drank a large swig as it was now the perfect temperature. "That is just what I needed...I'm freezing." Warmly dressed in her wool belted trench coat, infinity scarf, and knitted ear warmer headband the chill was still steadily apparent.

Tipping back his own half-drank cup he watched Clara as he did so. "So, what did you think?"

"Of the tree lighting? It was marvelous! I don't think I've ever seen that big a tree with so many lights. It's like there's an entire galaxy wrapped in its branches."

Auburn brows raised in surprise at her words. Nic grinned slowly in his appreciation. "I think that's a rather sexy way to describe a Christmas tree. Very poetic of you." Clara almost dropped her cup with how his voice dropped when he said "sexy". Flustered, she tried to find some semblance of words once again.

"Um, thank you." She chuckled shyly and huddled around her cup. "I guess it's the artist in me." Taking another quick swig, she was anxious to move on in the conversation lest she take him behind a tree in some dark corner of the park. "So...what's fun to do at this thing?"

Nic perked up at her question and he tried to hold back his flicker of excitement. "Well obviously... Ice skating." Nervous laughter spilled from her lips. Clara had only managed to go ice skating once and it...did not go well. All she could remember was holding onto the walls and how much pain she was in the next day.

"Oh...gosh. I'm terrible at ice skating." Clara stuttered, rather unsure at his suggestion.

"Maybe you just need to try again?" Nic offered hopefully. "You can just hold onto me."

With that mention, she was more than ready to jump wholeheartedly into his arms. "Well...maybe I can give it another shot. Are you as good a skating teacher as you are a knight?" She teased with a blush to her cheeks, and he nervously chuckled with her flirty sort of jest.

"As I've demonstrated before, I can come to your rescue. Even while I'm on ice." There was a playful wiggle to his brow as he was backing up in the direction of the makeshift rink while he tossed his empty cup. Downing the rest of her hot chocolate Clara followed after him with a giggling smile and disposed of her cup as well.

The two of them gave their sizes for the skates before Nic tutted away Clara's card to pay for her share of the admission and rental. Slipping her wallet back into her coat pocket, she smiled to herself and decided to pretend that this was something of a date. Her smile changed quickly when he turned to her with a pair of skates. The rink was busy but there were bare spots for them to at least attempt to maneuver on the ice.

Nic rose first and held out his hands to assist her in maneuvering over to the rink. Both of them had gloves on but the heat of his palms was undeniable as she slipped her fingers into his awaiting hands. She managed to stand and the pair locked gazes before her cursed ankle decided to give out causing her to stumble a bit.

Able to rise back up with minimal assistance, Clara brushed it off with laughter. "I'm off to a good start, aren't I?"

Firming up his grip on her forearms, Nic joined in with her laughter. "You'll be fine. Although you might be safer on the ice at this rate." He joked as they managed to maneuver themselves out onto the ice. Stepping onto the rink without even a breath of hesitation, Nic turned and reached out to her. "March onto the ice. Nice and easy."

Clara did as he asked and so far, so good. His feet moved subtly against the ice, very slowly and timidly skating backward as she continued to march. So far, no slipping and she was becoming more confident. It was wildly intimate to glide there on the ice, face to face. His eyes were an excellent distraction and he somehow avoided others on the ice with little effort.

"Okay keep one foot down and glide a bit. Then switch." His voice was soft and encouraging and Clara did as he said. Her leg wobbled a little but his grip on her tightened in reply and she felt much less scared. "See? You're doing great! Maybe one more lap and I'll move off to your side to help guide you." Clara's glide faltered slightly, and he moved a little closer to her as his brows furrowed in concentration. Nic was so close she could smell his cologne, some rich and deep scent of leather, and the outdoors. The scent made her knees give out slightly and he caught her, startling her a bit.

Chuckling, his palms were curled around her elbows and her hands had a vice grip on his forearms. "Concentrate, you've got it," Nic reassured her with a crooked grin as they rounded the last bend of the rink. "Look at you! You didn't fall."

"You've had a tight grip on me the whole time." Clara teased but was rather pleased with herself as she did manage to do one lap without much of a stumble. "It was helpful."

"How about we try side by side?" Gently, he adjusted his position as she looked on with minor concern. As soon as his hand slid across her back and around her side she lost all and any protest against the change. His left hand reached over to grasp hers. "Just lean on me." The tone of his voice had dropped to something hushed, and she couldn't help but stare at his lips for a long moment as she pressed up against him.

This was the closest the both of them had managed to be since the tree incident. Clara wanted nothing more than to stay exactly where he was holding her. Their eyes latched onto each other for a while as she continued the timid glide as he ushered her along. The cold around the both of them had become long forgotten as they eased through a few laps. There had only been a few hiccups, which Clara laughed off and he held her impossibly closer each time. Some part of her wanted to trip on purpose.

Circling the rink a few more times, Nic cleared his throat a bit before speaking. "Are you thirsty? Hungry? I think a break may be in order for all of our hard work."

Giggling softly, Clara nodded with a side-eye over at him. Apparently, most of the events revolving around both of them were food related. "Sure, that would be great." He guided her over to the exit and with only a minor bit of trouble, she was able to sit down and get the cursed skates off of her. Nic's tips had been extremely helpful, but she was feeling a bit stiff from the rigid way that she held herself as close as possible to him.

Upon returning their skates, the two of them wandered off to the various vendor huts that were set up and discussed the options. Not being able to agree on one thing, they both laughed and went their separate ways, promising to rendezvous in the same spot they parted from. Procuring each of their snacks and drinks, Nic gestured with his head to an empty park bench by the tree and they settled in.

"Thanks for inviting me," Clara murmured but caught herself. Did he technically invite her? It was more of an informative lead by him that she just happened to agree to. His pleasant laughter showed her he didn't notice the technicality.

"I'm glad you could make it. Maybe a new tradition for you?" Glancing over at Clara expectantly, he took a bite of his rather large gourmet cookie. Considering how that man looked shirtless, he either had the metabolism of an 8-year-old or worked out like a fiend. Her mind had wandered off on that tangent for a long moment before her eyes caught his looking at her.

"Oh…maybe. It is rather quaint. Like a little northern village. Although the ice skating might be once a season." Clara laughed her embarrassment away as she finished off her soft pretzel.

"Aww now…you did great! Nothing to worry about."

"Okay well, maybe I'll go again, but only with you." Her lashes dipped modestly with the stretch of a flirtation.

"No complaints from me." He shrugged, trying to be suave but his chest puffed with the words. Clara was open to hanging out again and he was here for it. The two of them finished off their snacks and drinks and she rose to start heading home. "Can I walk you to your car?" He offered with a hopeful tone.

"I mean technically you could...I actually walked here." Clara laughed bashfully as he rose up quickly to join her.

"Well, I know where you live...so can I walk you home instead?" He quipped right back with a vibrant grin, all too eager to continue the night together for as long as possible.

"Oh well, of course." Stepping in line next to her, they wandered down the sidewalk leading back to their homes. The noise of the festivities died off slowly as they walked in silence. She was admiring the Christmas lights along the street as the warm glow of the older street lights lit their path. There was silence, but it was not in the least bit uncomfortable.

Too enthralled by the sights of the decorations, Clara completely ignored the bank of black ice on the sidewalk in front of her. Immediately, she lost her footing. She felt that adrenaline rush as she flailed, trying to keep her balance. Nic was swift to react. He caught her with strong arms holding onto her waist, while hers had fallen to grasp tightly onto his shoulders. The look of surprise was still etched across her features while his were laced with concern.

"Are you okay?" With little effort, he righted her back up again and she was able to restart her breathing.

"Yes, thanks to you. Again." Smiling breathlessly, her eyes flitted over his face as it changed to a look of relief. "I'd probably still be driving around with my tree on my roof if it wasn't for you."

That pulled a rowdy laugh from him, and he shook his head at her humor. Noting how they still clutched at one another, his voice dropped to something a bit breathy. "I'm just glad I can continue to be your knight." Their eyes locked and for a long moment, her body went all rigid. Waiting for him to lean in, just a few inches more, and kiss her.

Unfortunately, Nic lost his nerve at the last moment. "Ah well…maybe it would be safer if I kept ahold of you, yes?" He offered with a subtle crack in his voice. Nodding vigorously and still breathless, he slowly slid his hands off of Clara and grasped onto her left hand before tucking it around his right arm. "Safety first." He chided with a lop-sided grin that sent her into a soft putter of giggles.

Squeezing his forearm reassuringly, the two of them set back down the sidewalk with eyes more focused on any more potential black ice. Gosh, she had missed this. This intimate yet innocent closeness with someone. Clara couldn't remember the last time that she took a man's arm on a borderline romantic walk. The cat-and-mouse guessing game that they were playing was growing somewhat tedious but with this closeness, she took her timid shot.

The top of her head just grazed the bottom of his nose, so she was the perfect height to lean in and rest her cheek against his shoulder as they walked. Now it was Nic's turn to stiffen and warm with her purely innocent hint of affection. Melting into her touch, he closed his eyes for a moment and just reveled in the feeling. Taking a chance himself, he reached up and placed his left hand atop hers on his forearm. Neither of them said anything, and neither of them mentioned it, but both of them absorbed every ounce of the warmth radiating between them.

Chapter Six

The night before, as they said their goodnights, Nic had managed to ask if it was okay if he could text her. The two of them ended up trading numbers and texting each other before bed. Nothing questionable, just goofy and sweet. He said it would be easier to figure out how the two of them could hang out more in the future.

Hang.

Out.

More.

Um…yes, please? Clara's mind was still reeling all of Monday, still reliving the entire night before. Nic had been such a gentleman, humorous and kind about the somewhat spontaneous outing. She had such a wonderful time. Honestly, it was the best first date (That technically wasn't a date?) that she had ever had.

Pulling into her driveway after work was a welcome relief from the day. Things were starting to die down with Christmas less than two weeks away. Although not anywhere near quick enough for her tastes. Clara was so thankful to be home. Walking up and onto her porch, she spied a unique bundle of a pile stacked on her rustic bench by the front door. Upon closer inspection, it was her wool throw she had loaned Nic from the weekend before, neatly folded. It was accompanied by her plastic containers, all freshly washed and stacked inside each other. To top it all off there was a lovely bouquet of evergreens and deep red roses.

Clara stood there in complete awe and surprise at the gift. Flowers? And such lovely flowers to boot, but also all her things returned in the loveliest and neatest pile.
Unlocking her front door, she quickly placed her laptop bag and purse down next to her foyer table before going back out to collect all the items from the porch.

Dropping the folded throw on the back of her couch, Clara brought the rest of the items into the kitchen to put away and fuss with. Grabbing her favorite vase, she gently unwrapped the lovely tissue paper from around the bouquet before adding water to the glass with the included flower food. Cutting the stems gingerly under the running water, she placed the grouping into the vase with a minor fluff. She wanted the arrangement front and center, so she placed it on the coffee table with a warm smile.

Okay…so Nic was just so completely amazing. Flowers were a sure sign of something…right? Right? She couldn't remember a time when male/female neighbors surprised each other with flowers, just because. Lost in her fretting, she wandered back over to the folded throw and unfurled it. Clara was immediately struck with the faint scent of his cologne, and she almost melted into a puddle on the floor. Whelp. She knew she was snuggling with that night.

Glancing at her phon,e she almost had the guts to text Nic to come over and…stay over. This tedious yet delicious game of give and take was driving her mad. As much as her body was desperate for his, she was still obnoxiously hesitant. One-night stands were never really her thing. Sex was great and all, but it was much more fun when there was some kind of established relationship and an acceptable comfort level.

Almost as if he was on the same wavelength, her phone buzzed with a text alert from Nic. She startled slightly and then bit her lip in a vain effort to stall her smile.

Want to get together on Saturday?

38

Unfortunately, it's the first time I'm free all week

    With a groan, Clara picked up her phone to contemplate her answer. It just so happened to be that one Saturday a month that she volunteered at the library for story time. She hadn't missed a day since she started volunteering a few months ago. She had a silly holiday book picked out and she was really looking forward to how many giggles she could get out of the audience.

Sure! I'll have to let you know when though. I'm doing story time at the library at 11. The munchkins usually coerce me into reading more than one

Isn't that cute
Let me know when they release you from their custody

I will :)
Thank you for the flowers. They made my day

Just a small token of my return thanks
The stew and biscuits were just as good as the first time

I'm glad you enjoyed everything!
It's nice to cook for someone
Let me know if you need a cookie refill ;)

    The two of them texted on and off throughout the evening and continued through the rest of the week. Texts were sent at random times, whenever either of them could steal a few seconds away from work or other household obligations. Since it seemed that they had perhaps a proper date coming up, the words tumbled out with greater ease and they both learned more things about each other. Of course, now that Clara had something fun to look forward to, the week was going to drag on endlessly.

Chapter Seven

By some miracle, Saturday finally arrived. Clara left her home a bit early so she could walk to the local library and find the books she wanted to read to the younglings. As expected, the children's story time was a hit and they managed to convince her to read four additional books from the three she had wanted to read. There were fits of giggles and calling out and just overall fun interactions. It made the whole volunteering experience more than worthwhile. Since Clara had been volunteering for so long, she had quite a "fan" base with the younglings.

The children protested for more, but she had to call it. They had already managed to pull an entire hour of her and some of the parents were looking rather antsy. As the crowd had begun to disperse, Clara bent to gather her things. A delectable voice sounded from over her shoulder.

"Hello there."

The flush of surprise was immediate, and she quickly turned around and couldn't help the bright smile.

"Nic! Stopping by for a book?" She peaked a brow at him with her question, trying to figure out why we would just so happen to be there at the library as she finished volunteering.

"Ah…well no. I come for story time. It's pretty entertaining." His grin was wry and impish, and her cheeks erupted in a bloom of embarrassment.

"Oh my god, please tell me you didn't watch that nonsense…"

"Why not? It was rather adorable." Shoving his hands into the pockets of his jeans he shuffled his feet. "Heck I was probably more amused than some of the kids."

Clara couldn't help but giggle at that. The fact that he was still talking to her after that overly theatrical performance was a good sign that her utter goofiness didn't scare him away. Yet.

"Ah well...thanks." In a desperate attempt to hide her rattling fluster she draped her coat over her arm and gathered her purse.

"So..." Nic was trying to hide his nervousness with his subtle fidgeting. "Would you like to grab lunch?"

"Oh..." A warm smile fluttered to Clara's lips as she hugged her coat against her chest. "I'd love to. But...do you think I can peruse the library a bit? I have some books that I'm looking for. They'll keep me distracted over the quiet Christmas break from work." She shrugged, doing her best not to sound super lonely and desperate.

"No problems here. I don't think I ever had the chance to check out the library yet, so this is a good excuse." Chuckling, he nodded and followed after her as she was very well acquainted with the place. Clara scanned the shelves, looking for her list of books that she was planning on reading over her first major holiday alone. It was going to be somewhat unpleasant, but she planned a video chat with her parents, a marathon of Christmas movies, and all her favorite snacks.

The lovely older ladies at the library were so sweet as they decorated the facility for every holiday. Each section was decorated in its own little theme. Clara took her time admiring the decor as she looked for books. Nic followed somewhat close behind. He found himself getting lost in reviewing the spines and opening a few books to read the synopsis.

Clara was at the tail end of the Romance section when some of her little friends from story time were checking out their books and preparing to leave.

"Hiya miss!" One shouted at her and she turned with a warm smile and a laugh. "I got the book you read!"

Bending down a bit to get down on her level, Clara looked down at the pile that the child held up for her inspection. "Oh, I see! Did you like it?"

"You are so funny when you read these. My mommy isn't as good as you." Clara winced slightly from behind her now strained grin. Glancing at the mom with an apologetic look, she shrugged with a laugh.

"Oh well...uh...maybe you need to read them to her like me?" The little girl's eyes lit up with that suggestion and she looked at their mom with an excited grin. "I hope you have a nice holiday."

Bouncing, the youngling smashed her pile of books in a fierce hug to her chest as her eyes sparkled. "Mommy...ain't that missile toad?" She pointed to something right above Clara's head and she froze for a moment. The little girl said it with a slight lisp, but she didn't mistake what the child meant. As if on cue Clara and Nic slowly both looked up, a wild mix of excitement and apprehension as they both spotted the unmistakable branch with white berries that were hanging from a red velvet bow.

"Oh, it is!" The mom said with a smile and patted her daughter on the shoulder with a laugh.

To make the situation even more awkward, the little girl jumped up excitedly. "Miss you gotta kiss him." She jutted her thumb to Nic, looking rather forlorn. "It's the law! That's what mommy says when she's under it with daddy!" It was now the mother's turn to be rather embarrassed and she began to steer her child away from the two of them and headed out the door.

They both were staring at the mistletoe as they were now left alone. The thudding of Clara's beating heart was rampant in her chest.

"Well..." The two of them turned to face one another rather unknowingly. "You heard the little one." Nic's words were soft from within a half-smile of amusement, barely

43

above a husky whisper. Clara's eyes moved immediately to meet his, which were now gazing at her with anticipation. "It is the law…"

The draw together was unhurried, with only the slightest bit of hesitation. Considering how quickly they both assumed the position with one simple demand, it was safe to believe that it was wanted. They were relieved by the excuse, as neither of them seemed to have the gumption to make the first move. Lips met in the softest and most tender caress, and Clara felt the onslaught of warmth overwhelm her. His touch was impossibly amorous, and she could have easily spent the rest of the day locked in this embrace.

There was a subtle clearing of the throat from the one librarian who slipped the pair a knowing smile, but people were starting to stare. Clara glanced at Nic. He looked rather flustered himself and there was a pink tinge on his cheeks that matched hers.

Awkwardly, he cleared his throat and moved his eyes from hers, trying to hide his smile. "Um…so…uh lunch?"

Biting her bottom lip, she nodded but couldn't help the curl of her lips. "It's a date." Clara wasn't exactly sure where that bold word choice came from, but she was not regretting it in the least bit after that kiss. "Just um…let me check out these books first?"

"Oh…sure… I'll just be outside." Nodding, Nic stepped back slowly to allow her to head to the front desk to scan her pile. With Clara's back turned to him, he grinned like mad. His heart still fluttered about in the aftermath as he stepped through the automatic doors. Nic was thankful for the reprieve and space away from her for a minute. He needed to gather his thoughts and not make an embarrassing ass of himself while still lost in his fluster.

Clara stepped outside shortly after, arranging the books in her large tote of a purse that she had specifically brought for the day. Nic was all bundled back up and continuing to fidget in his wait. She took whatever moment she could to admire the man. The kiss left her body still reeling. So desperately she wanted to talk to him about it, anxious to know if he was feeling anything remotely similar to what she was.

Hearing Clara approach, he turned and smiled at her with that same brilliant smile that hadn't seemed to fade in the least bit from their kiss.

"So...I was thinking the cafe just around the corner would be good? We can walk." Swallowing hard, he suppressed his apprehension and extended his hand to her. Without any hesitation, Clara took it with a shy smile, clasping onto his bare hand with relish and the utmost satisfaction. The skin-to-skin contact was delightful and helped her forget the chill so much that she didn't mind being ungloved.

The two of them walked in silence down the somewhat busy town center street. With the increase in foot traffic from the holiday shopping, Clara had to press herself in close against him to cram onto one side of the sidewalk. Squeezing her hand a little tighter, he pulled her in without a thought as they meandered to the cafe. It was bustling at the lunch hour, but they were able to score the last little bistro table for two in the corner.

Hanging their coats up on the rack nearby, they settled in with shy smiles from across the table. There was a lingering silence between them, still slightly unsure how they could continue talking about anything after such an intimate moment.

Nic broke first with a bashful dip of his chin and looked up at Clara through hooded lashes. "I have to say... I've been wanting to kiss you for a long time."

"Oh..." She breathed out in some wild mix of relief and utter delight. "I...me too."

His warm chuckle broke the tension, and she couldn't help but smile. Clara was about to add to it, but the waitress slid in next to the table to take their order. Handing off the menu and a thankful smile to the waitress, she turned to put in their orders. Nic seized the moment of Clara's distraction.

Reaching across the table he took her right hand into his and pressed a warm kiss to her knuckles as his mouth and eyes both smiled at her.

God help this man. He was lucky that it was a busy restaurant or else Clara may have tackled him across the small table. The touch was vibrantly enticing. She felt the flush of heat rise up her torso to her cheeks from deep within her core. He was leaning in towards her, with elbows on the table and looking so effortlessly handsome with his ruffled auburn hair and V-neck claret-colored sweater. There was a teasing peek of his white undershirt through the neckline, and she felt herself wilt even more.

"This…this feels nice." Clara breathed out and blushed again as she took his lead and leaned onto the table. Lips moved in a soft caress against her fingertips, careful to touch each one as his eyes stayed on hers.

"I'm not sure I'll ever get enough of it now." With a subtle twist of his wrist, he tipped her hand back and placed a lingering kiss on the inside of her wrist. "Now that I've had a taste of it." Clara's eyes widened with the sudden rush of desire, and she subconsciously bit down on her lower lip in a vain effort to suppress it.

The waitress saved the other patrons of the cafe from something rather lewd. She broke the two of them apart by placing their plates down in front of each of them. Staring at her food for a long moment, Clara was both thankful for the reprieve and somewhat annoyed. At least now she could try to recenter herself after all the rather intimate touches that were occurring suddenly between them.

Clearing her throat. Clara busied herself with cutting up her meal. "So, I…uh don't think I ever asked you what you're doing for Christmas? It's only a few days away."

Nic looked rather sheepish and just shrugged as he absentmindedly stabbed at some food on his plate. "Well...probably the usual. Chinese food, action movies, and trying to get my email inbox to zero."

Clara's heart jumped to her throat, as she stared at her food, quickly trying to formulate a plan from his words. "Oh well…do you want to come over for Christmas…?" The words were rather timid. Her gaze slid up to gauge his reaction as her chin was still dipped toward her plate. "My family can't manage the trip to visit, and well…I can't either. So, all I was planning on was reading, watching Christmas movies, and eating lots of snacks."

Pausing and trying to keep his poker face straight, Nic contemplated the invitation. Immediately he wanted to say yes. Nothing in that moment sounded better than spending it with a wildly attractive woman whom he had just shared a beyond memorable kiss with. He just had to play it cool instead of completely enveloping her in his arms with the utmost thanks for her thoughtfulness.

"Actually…" He paused as he lifted his head to fully drink Clara in. "That sounds a hell of a lot better."

A breathless smile immediately lit her face. She sat up in her chair, trying to suppress the rest of her excitement.

"Okay, well…great!" It wasn't the smoothest of responses, but it got the job done. The rest of their lunch was spent zealously planning for their time together on Christmas eve and Christmas. Deciding to split the duties, Nic would take care of the snack fest for Christmas eve and Clara would handle the dinner for Christmas. Well and the desserts, at Nic's insistence.

The planning continued the entire walk home, even including an epic holiday movie lineup for Christmas eve. Nic had reached for her hand as soon as they left the restaurant. It was as if it was now second nature and Clara accepted it without an ounce of hesitation this time as they both enjoyed the leisurely walk down the street. The two of them stayed close, with arms brushing against each other constantly as they both spoke with such ease and delight. Christmas was suddenly going to be so much more exciting.

Nic followed her up the stoop and Clara paused with her key in hand before turning to him with a demure smile. "Can I say this was the best Saturday I've ever had?"

Chuckling softly, he pressed closer to her, and Clara backed up against the door frame with a bite to her lower lip from the advance. "I had a great time. With even more to look forward to." His voice dropped with every word as his intense cerulean gaze fell to study her mouth.

Clara's grin was slow. She was ready with some kind of acknowledging retort, but his hand was already cupping her face with a brush of his thumb across her cheekbone. The touch scared off all words, spoken or unspoken, as he dipped his head down to capture her mouth.

This time the kiss was deep and pressing. His whole body molded against hers so enticingly close that the heat between them was almost stifling. Clara was quickly melting like butter put too close to a burning flame. Without the hesitation of being in a public space, the pressure easily went a bit sultrier. With a tilt of his head, his lips caressed hers and she felt the subtle tease of his tongue.

"Finally!" There was a relieved shout from the yard. They froze with a deer-in-the-headlights stare at each other while their lips were still locked. Nic pulled away from Clara quickly and turned to look towards the street. The neighbor, Mrs. Fitz, was standing on the sidewalk at the end of the front path, taking her dog for a walk. "It's about time you two did something." She grumbled with a rumpled grin before continuing on her way.

With a look over his shoulder, Nic brought his hand to his mouth with his incredulous embarrassment and muffled laughter. His face made Clara immediately crack up into a snort and endless bubbling giggles. Turning to her fully, he shook his head in his exasperation as he stepped back in close.

"Sorry…" He muttered bashfully in between his laughter. "She's been trying to get me to ask you out since you moved in."

Clara was startled slightly in surprise before erupting into more incredulous giggles. "Oh…really?" Her manicured brow peaked high on her forehead. She found it only somewhat difficult to believe that the sweet old lady next door was trying to hook them up. "I thought she was just enjoying watching our month-long escapade of awkwardness like some odd neighborhood soap opera."

With a shake of his head, he laughed. "No…just an awkward attempt to be my matchmaker."

Clara's other brow met the first and the two furrowed with her surprise as her fingers played with the collar of his coat. "Well…did it work?"

"Technically…" He leaned in quickly and the prolonged kiss left her completely breathless with its sudden force and a smile behind it. "It did."

Chapter Eight

Clara had done it.

She finally managed to kiss her knight-in-shining-armor neighbor.

And the kiss?

Oh, those kisses had been divine. Once the coast had been clear, Nic had stolen a few more before reluctantly heading home. The early afternoon together had extended well into the early evening. He finally stepped off her front porch around twilight. That sultry side of her was dying to wrap her arms around his neck and drag him inside the house to see what would happen. Except the two of them just had their first (of many) kisses. Most people don't typically go from the first kiss to straight-up sex in the same day. Well…at least Clara didn't quite feel comfortable with that.

Yet.

Thankfully, Christmas was just a few days away and she and Nic had agreed to wrap up what they could at work while prepping for their little Christmas get-together. If Clara hadn't had anything else to occupy her time until then, then she probably would have ended up marching over to his apartment and locking herself inside with him. It was still torture to wait, but the sweet texts back and forth were a welcome reprieve as she dove into her holiday preparations.

The two of them had settled on Christmas Eve at Nic's and Christmas Day at Clara's. It was a rather fair exchange as they both needed to tidy up their places and make some sort of a meal. Encouraged by Nic's endless compliments about her cooking, she was in the mood for the traditional kind of holiday feast. Complete with ham, potatoes, biscuits, green beans, and the rest of her horde of cookies. No sense in keeping them around after Christmas.

Nic had been rather secretive about his plans but had reassured Clara that it would be fun, and she'd love it. She was curious as to what he had in store. He was full of good ideas and had been rather clever and thoughtful with how he managed to surprise her throughout the time she'd known him.

Speaking of surprises Clara cursed herself mid-email. Were they expected to get each other gifts? Was it going to be expected? Appreciated? Honestly, she'd be happy if he walked out into the living room wearing nothing but a bow. That gift would certainly be greatly appreciated.

Feeling a sudden hot flash, Clara quickly finished and sent the email before closing her laptop for the day. Settling back into the plush confines of her couch she closed her eyes for a moment. The quiet reprieve welcoming quiet reprieve from the workday was welcome. The image of a rather naked Nic was entertaining her thoughts. Ever since the first encounter with the man, she had spent almost every night remembering how he felt under her touch. All warm and firm with easily distinguishable curvature of his muscles all throughout his arms and torso.

Nic's touch had been a constant comfort, even the subtle and passing ones. Some brought the heat, and some made her feel impossibly safe. Clara couldn't stop thinking about him. He was the entire package of being extremely attractive, kind, endearing, and funny. All while being ever so down to earth. It was a wonder he was still single. What she could tell is that he was more involved with work than going out of his way to find love. He was confident and comfortable with himself. She adored that about him.

Of course, her mind kept sliding to the thoughts of his kisses and her body started to percolate once more. If that man made love half as good as he kissed, Clara would be set for life. It's not like she hadn't imagined having sex with the man. She did. Almost daily. How that lithe body would feel pressing her into the mattress, moving together in the darkness of a chilly winter's night. Maybe he likes to be teasing, slow, and drawn out to keep the sex going for hours. Or maybe he becomes unhinged and needs to absorb one all at once in a ravishment of kisses and caresses. Either way, she had a feeling that she would be completely satisfied.

Clara was borderline panting at this point, working herself up with her daydream to something of a frenzy. She needed to find something else to distract herself. If she kept up this torture, she might end up tackling the man as soon as he opened the door on Christmas Eve. Not that she would have an issue. It's just that he might.

Deciding to put the brainstorming about a possible gift on the back burner, she set about planning her timing for how she would go about preparing Christmas dinner. Clara wanted as little as possible to do on Christmas morning, so it was all about the pre-prep. Perhaps it was worth getting the slow cooker out again for the ham and making all of the sides beforehand. Except for the mashed potatoes, they were always better fresh.

Clara's home was already tidy from her cleanup session on Friday. She debated giving her bedroom the full once-over, just in case Nic might happen to make his way in there…in one way or another. She was still locked in an endless debate over that. Why go through all the effort to get her hopes up for nothing? It was overdue for a thorough clean though. Maybe that was something she could do Christmas Eve before heading over to Nic's

The plan was to go over around 5 pm for dinner, movies, and dessert. They had settled on two different movies, one selection from each of their favorites. Despite how short of a time Clara had known the man, she was looking forward to back-to-back days of his smile in her life. The Christmas Day plans were for him to come over around 12 pm for the traditional Christmas feast with dessert. Maybe some games and movies as well, she hadn't quite decided yet. She wanted to keep him entertained for as long as possible so he would not want to go home until very late in the evening.

Or at all.

Chapter Nine

It was impossibly dark when Clara walked up the steps to Nic's second-floor apartment. Twilight had faded into the depth of the evening and the entire street was now aglow from the Christmas lights lined up and down the streets. A slow fluff of snow had started to fall just before she made her way over. She was sure to don her ankle snow boots just in case for a careful walk home later. It was the picturesque quintessential Christmas Eve.

Clara couldn't go to Nic's empty-handed so she had filled up a smaller container full of her over-abundance of cookies, knowing they would be greatly appreciated. Considering this a date, she had managed to put on a light layer of makeup and curled her hair into very loose tendrils that fell down along her back. He had insisted that this was going to be a very informal thing. She dressed in her black and white plaid, impossibly soft flannel feminine-cut blouse and skinny jeans. Simple studs sparkled upon the lobe of her ears and were the little sparkling touch that her outfit needed.

Hesitating at his front door, she shifted the container of cookies between her hands. Her earlier fluster had come back in force, and she needed to desperately talk herself down off the edge. This was going to be a night of casual fun.

Knocking softly, Nic answered the door immediately, as if he had been standing there waiting for Clara to arrive. He was wearing a dark blue dress shirt that was effortlessly untucked and unbuttoned at the top collar. There was a delightful peek of skin between the dip of his clavicle and bare forearms, with his sleeves rolled up to the elbows. She felt herself swallow down the heat that was simmering over all too quickly. Her eyes slipped to the peek of naked skin immediately for a quick glance before moving up to his grinning face.

His left hand was nervously shoved into his jeans pocket as he held the door open for her. Clara stood there for a moment, unsure and slightly uneasy about what to do next as he closed the door behind her. Nic didn't hesitate in the least bit. As soon as the door latched closed, he was cupping her face and brushing a kiss against her mouth before a greeting could even be uttered.

A slow exhale of warm air escaped Clara while she reveled in the kiss. All while awkwardly holding the container of cookies between them both.

"Hey." She breathed, the smile on her face addled by the kiss.

"Hey." He grinned right back and finally gave her some space. "Sorry, it's the law after all." Cerulean blue eyes flickered up and Clara's followed the course. She erupted in utter laughter at the sight of mistletoe hanging right above them.

"Was that…always there?" she asked with a questioning raise of her brow as she handed him the cookies before taking off her coat to hang on a vacant hook by the door. Toeing off her boots she made sure they found their way onto his shoe tray as the snow was already beginning to melt from them.

Turning to the rest of the living room, he placed the container of cookies on the coffee table that had already been completely set for the evening.

"Well…no. That was an impulse buy after Saturday." Shoulder shrugged sheepishly as he moved his eyes to survey the spread that he had laid out one last time. Laughing, Clara smiled to herself as she gave a quick sweep of the room with her eyes. He had managed to string Christmas lights all around the room and it felt like they were surrounded by the stars. It cast a warm glow over everything and between those and the Christmas tree, they were the only lights in the room.

The coffee table and couch had been cleaned off and tidied of his work mess. Which made way for quite the impressive charcuterie board paired with a bottle of wine and two glasses. It all looked too pretty to be eaten. After prepping all day for the meal tomorrow, Clara was starving.

"Wow…this looks absolutely amazing." Her eyes lifted to his with some question, but she was going to be greatly impressed either way. "Did you do all this?"

"Well, I had to at least attempt to one-up you. I found a few good online tutorials and thought I could give it a shot."

Impressed by his fortitude, Clara had wandered over to admire his artistic handiwork. Crossing her arms as she leaned in to review the delicacies. "It's almost too pretty to eat." Looking up, she beamed at him and noted the softest hint of blush on his cheeks before he laughed.

"You'd better eat it! It took me all afternoon to set it up." He insisted as he moved to open the bottle of wine and fill the two glasses. "So, sit down and help yourself." A soft smile stayed on his lips as he handed her a glass. Grabbing the remote, he queued up the movie on the television hanging on the wall behind him. Clara did as he asked, taking a long draw from her glass as she was quite parched after that sudden kiss in welcome.

The soundtrack of the movie flooded the speakers as the opening title sequence was winding up. Satisfied with setting up the mood, Nic discarded the remote on the coffee table and made his way to the couch to sit down next to her. Quickly grabbing his glass, he held it up in offering.

"Happy Christmas Eve." His smile was warm but flickered with the tell-tale signs of relief as he was more than delighted to not spend the holiday alone. The bonus was that it was Clara he was spending it with.

Clinking her glass to his, she responded, "Happy Christmas Eve, Nic. I'm glad we could figure all this out."

There was a quiet moment as they both timidly sipped the wine. "It's been quite the gift getting to know you these past few weeks."

"The feeling is very mutual." Nic chuckled as he reached out for a piece of cheese. "Usually, I don't do much outside the ordinary at this time of the year. But this year…this year you made it seem like magic." Clara's smile was warm with only a slight tremble to her lower lip. The last few weeks had been magical. Nic had managed to draw her out of her shell. He helped her make some wonderful memories of what would have been her first Christmas alone.

With the opening scene well established, the two of them settled into the delightful array of snacks he had laid out. It was a lovely setup but seemed so effortless and delicious, perfect for the casual evening he had planned. The best spread for their low-key holiday celebration. Nic had settled in close to her, their bodies almost touching as they sat side-by-side.

Every now and then Clara would settle back into the plushness of the couch after putting her wine glass on the table. His hand would flex on his thigh, almost as if he was in a debate about something. The third time she sat back with a handful of goodies, Nic slid his arm across the back of the couch so that it was perched right above her shoulders. It was so nonchalant as he kept his eyes glued to the screen as he did it. Almost as if he was trying to play it off as a reflex.

It wasn't until Clara scooted herself over to close the gap that his arm draped down around her shoulders. She could almost feel the sigh of relief he released as she did so, now perfectly content with their situation. His fingers spread out and draped over the curve of her shoulder, teasing the breadth of her bicep now and then. The touch was incredibly soothing, and his prolonged closeness helped her completely relax against him.

By the time the first movie drew to a close, the two of them had managed to devour most of the charcuterie board. Only leaving behind a few stray crackers and some grapes.

Nic was on his second glass of wine as he munched on a cookie. He grabbed another while he reached for the remote. Clara couldn't help but chuckle at him with half a snowflake cooking hanging out of his mouth, making his one cheek protrude like a chipmunk.

Catching her staring and laughing, Nic tried to feign some kind of innocence as he managed a garbled and muffled, "What?"

"You look like you're trying to forage for winter." She teased as she continued her laughter. He managed to finish off the rest of the first cookie and easily munched through the second.

"So, what if I am? Stop making delicious cookies." Grinning around the last bite of the arm of the snowflake, he crunched down on it before taking a sip of his wine. Placing the glass back down on the coffee table, he subtly adjusted his body to face more toward Clara. His knee pressed against her thigh. Propping his elbow against the back of the couch and leaning his cheek against his fisted hand, his eyes washed over her face in muted appreciation.

Now it was her turn to ask the question. "What?" Clara's fingers rose to brush across her mouth, ensuring that she didn't have any lingering semblance of a snack anywhere.

"You're the most amazing woman I've ever met." His voice was hushed, awed almost. He watched her face flash over with a blush and a demure dip of her lashes with her timidness. Clara dropped her hand to her thigh, and he immediately enveloped it with his left hand before his other joined it. There was a protest budding on her parted lips and before she could utter anything, he brought her knuckles to his mouth and kissed them. "Truly."

That impossibly slow-burning heat was back, swirling low in her belly, and was now haltingly infiltrating her bloodstream. He moved her hand into his lap, still clasped within both of his. He dropped his head into the plushness of the back of the sofa and now admired Clara with sparkling cerulean eyes from a cockeyed tilted angle with that same dreamy smile.

Biting her bottom lip, Clara hesitated for a long moment as she took the time to revere the way his sharp and freshly shaven jawline jutted up toward her. The delightful dimple in the center of his chin was front and center and she wanted nothing more than to kiss it. Her body made a move first, even before her brain could argue otherwise. Slipping her hand from his grasp it joined her other to cup the hard edge of his jaw, just underneath his ears, to keep his head right where she wanted it.

For just a moment her eyes caught his and Clara could see the desperate fire within. Rising up on her knees just a tad, she tipped her head and captured his eager mouth. It all seemed like it was happening in slow motion, but the advances were breathlessly fluid and quick. After days apart their mouths were ravenous to absorb one another. Her hands slid from their hold against his face, maneuvering their way around his neck to pull him into a fierce embrace.

Feeling Clara's eagerness, Nic moved his torso away from the back of the couch. She settled back to sit on her feet but now he was free to fiercely curl his arms around her. Sighing into his mouth, she could feel his tongue caress her barely parted lips. With a shiver, she coaxed him inside with a greeting of her own tongue. Her fingers tangled in his mussed auburn locks along the back of his head. Mouths danced together while their tongues were thrown into the mix. The desperation level was quickly rising as they both felt the unyielding need to be closer to one another.

Pressing him against the back of the sofa, Clara slowly maneuvered herself without releasing her lips from Nic's, to timidly straddle his lap. There was some sort of low approving rumble deep in his chest from her undertaking. She felt that numbing heat begin to flood her system. Her arms untangled from around his neck to scrape down the breadth of his chest, questing over and absorbing the feel of the ridges of his muscles beneath the fabric. Her bottom finally settled down onto his thighs and his hands moved to grip her hips.

Nic's hands were as firm and frank as Clara's, sliding down from her hips to the outside of her thighs to leave a trail of fire in their wake. His touch across new places caused her to arch her pelvis in an unspoken desperation toward him. The groan that tumbled into her mouth made every synapse of skin prickle and her fingers curled into the fabric of his neatly pressed dress shirt. His hands furiously raked their way back up her thighs to cup the roundness of her bottom with a firm squeeze.

With his touch, she couldn't help but rock her hips against his and she felt that enticing hardness. Wildly frenzied now, his hands snuck up and slid under the back hem of her flannel blouse. Impossibly hot hands grazed against the bare skin of her lower back and a sharp gasp escaped her mouth. His hands against her skin felt enthralling but he suddenly hesitated with her reaction.

"I...I'm sorry..." Nic panted as he reluctantly pulled away from her mouth, blinking as if awoken from a trance. Clara felt the loss of his mouth and hands immediately and her eyes flashed open in confusion.

"...For what?" she asked, still in quite a daze herself.

"I was...I was being entirely too forward." Those enchanting blue eyes took a shy turn.

"What? That...that's silly." Pulling back from him only slightly, she ran her fingers through her hair. Clara was feeling rather exasperated but still extremely wanting. "This is literally the hottest make out session I've ever had." The words tumbled out in one quick breath, but it was just the thing that broke the tension that had settled between them.

Shaking hands reached for her face. The pads of his thumbs caressed her cheekbones as he pulled her lips to his. The kiss was of breathless relief, and he instantly devoured her mouth. Just as quickly as he pulled her in, he was uttering hushed words in between fierce kisses.

"Really?" His all-encompassing mouth had moved to her jaw before placing searing hot, open-mouthed kisses down the length of her neck. "But I…" Clara felt the swirl of his tongue between his lips and her mouth dropped open, noiselessly gasping with the ravishing of his mouth. "I was hoping we could do more…"

The pressure between her legs was so close to bursting at his sultry admission. Her hands had been hovering in midair until that moment, unsure and hopeful that this would continue. Right now, she wanted nothing more than to grant his wish.

"I was thinking you'd never ask." The words were rasping out into the night air as her fingers swiftly maneuvered to the buttons on her shirt, slipping the pearly rounds through the slots one by one. Nic's appreciative mouth soon followed, chasing after them, as it had been paying homage to the dip at the base of her throat.

There was an appreciative moan against her sternum, and she shivered with the implications. His tremoring fingers slipped back under the hem of Clara's shirt along her sides. They hover just above the waist of her jeans, anxious for her to finish her unbuttoning. Timid now, his lips only grazed against her skin as his eyes waited for that one last button to be released.

The moment her shirt fell open, Nic pulled away so he could admire you fully. Bashful fingers moved to her collar, and he gently nudged it over the curve of her shoulders. The flannel fabric slid down her biceps to pool at the crook of her elbows, leaving a tide of goosebumps in its wake. Clara couldn't help the blush on her already flushed cheeks as those wild cerulean eyes raked over every inch of her.

"You are so… exquisitely beautiful." The words were impossibly soft, almost as if they were exhaled into the small gap of air between them. Clara's eyes dipped demurely with a tip of her chin. A curled finger reached to nudge her jaw back up so Nic could meet her eyes once again. The same

61

finger moved to bring her back to his lips. Nic drank her in slowly, a tender sweep of his mouth across hers. Melting against him, her torso pressed into his and his hands moved to fondle all the freshly revealed skin.

There was a subtle shift beneath her as Nic scooted himself to the edge of the sofa. His hands and forearms reached under her to cup and support her bottom and thighs. He managed to stand while holding her against him. Clara's legs instinctively wrapped around his waist as her hands grasped him around his neck with a gasp of surprise. He continued to steal quick kisses as he carefully maneuvered his way around the coffee table.

Clara was completely breathless at this point, hopeful of where he was taking her, but she still needed to be sure. "Wh-where are we going…?"

"I want to lay you out so I can ravish you properly." His accented voice was husky, so sure, and determined as he transported her down the darkened hallway to his bedroom. Clara trembled with his erotic admission and there was nothing on the entire planet that was sexier than his words. She gripped him more tightly, as he managed to stumble into his room. Every synapse of her body was desperately hoping that he was going to be true to his promise.

Chapter Ten

With the utmost care, Clara was placed onto the plush bedding of his bed. Nic remained standing, his gaze drifting over her and committing this moment to the deepest recesses of his memories. Fingers quickly moved to tend to the first few buttons of his own shirt before dipping his hands back behind his head and between his shoulder blades to grasp at his shirt and pull it up over. The sweep of the dress shirt against his hair ruffled it playfully but she hardly noticed as she was in full absorption of the glorious view of his toned chest.

When he had come to her rescue the first time, Clara did her best to avoid staring straight at the finely sculpted skin. As for right now, she was drinking in every last morsel of the view, knowing that she was just moments away from completely devouring all of him. His intense stare stayed on her as she shrugged off the remains of her top and tossed it over the edge of the bed. While Clara was distracted, his fingers were maneuvering the belt through the buckle and the movement was shifting the denim against the hardness beneath.

Nic's jeans hit the floor before she could even manage to get the button for her fly through the hole. With his one knee up on the bed, Clara stilled, watching him with wide and yearning eyes. Leaning in towards her, she gently laid herself back with his advance, eyes intently locked on hers. His body moved to cover hers, molding his hard corners against her delicious curves.

There was only a moment of stillness before his mouth captured hers, voraciously succumbing to the touch. Clara's fingers tangled in his mess of auburn before his hands managed to slip between them both to finish unfastening her jeans. His fingers dipped below the loosened waistband to wrestle the fabric down over her hips. Noting the slight awkwardness of trying to remove the denim from her with him on top, his body began its teasing descent down her body.

Kisses were soft and fervid, following the trail of her sternum to down between the heaving mounds of her breasts. His nose nuzzled against the dark lace as he continued down the path. With a hot breath, his lips were tickling around her navel as his hands were able to tug her jeans down to her knees. He persisted as the fabric slipped off her feet, the flit of his tongue dipping below the waist of her panties.

Clara's mind was a fierce tumble of thoughts all at once. She did manage to thank herself for spending that extra hour on some more intense grooming than her usual routine. Now that his hands were free, they enticingly slid up the bared skin of her legs causing a shiver to run up her spine. Once his hands met up with his mouth, he ascended back up to recapture her lips with a vengeance. Her hands immediately sprang into action, raking down and across his chest, eager to trace every inch of the muscle that flexed above her.

Nic had all the fun undressing, and now Clara wanted to have her turn. Bending her knees up to cradle his hips, she was able to press her palms against his chest to roll him onto his back. Now it was him who had the questioning look of surprise across his handsome face as she settled herself down, straddling his pelvis. Her eyes soaked in the vision beneath her. Nic was breathless, flushed, and borderline desperate to have all of her. The look he gave her only encouraged her along more.

Shifting her arms behind her back, Clara's fingers deftly loosened the hooks and eyes causing the shoulder straps of her bra to slacken. She let it sit there against her skin with his eyes becoming more anxious by the second. Moving her fingers up to her shoulders, she coaxed the straps down and off, tossing the garment onto the floor. His eyes widened to an impossible degree as they gazed earnestly at the enticing curve of her breasts.

Sitting straight up, his hands delicately reached out to encompass the warm orbs with a completely tender caress. Clara couldn't help but close her eyes with a soft sigh of delight, letting him take pleasure in his slow conquest of her naked body. Bending down, he cupped the heft of one and brought it to his lips. Paying sweet homage to the skin and across her nipple, eliciting the daintiest mewl from her mouth. Her nails raked down his back in a vain effort to try to pull him closer to her.

It was then that he cradled the span of her naked back with his palms and pressed Clara back against the mattress with a kiss that took her breath away. This was quickly becoming a sensual game of give and take, each one of them breaking quicker and harder with every turn. Keeping him deep in the depths of her kiss, her hands moved to cup his length, still trapped inside his dark boxer briefs. Maybe one day she could admire him wandering around his apartment in nothing but those. For right now, right now she needed to strip him of his last remaining article of clothing.

The groan penetrated deep into her mouth, sending heat across her tongue as it tangled with his. Nic was so incredibly hard already from the prolonged evening of the slow burn between them both. Reaching down ever so timidly, Clara slipped her fingers into the waistband of his boxers. She felt his stomach concave in from the elicit contact. Too quick to allow him much more of a reaction than that, her teasing fingers stretched out across his skin to trace his length. Nic's fingers dug helplessly into the bedding, strangling the cotton in his grasp.

With a subtle twist of her wrist, Clara laid out her searing hot palm against him. Her breath hitched as she slid her curled fist from the base to the tip, noting the delightful heft and spread of his desire. She had no idea that he was this pleasurably large and she bit her lower lip with the implication. He had unsteadily propped himself up on his balled fists, pulling away from her mouth to catch his breath as she become surer and firmer with her stroking.

The way Nic looked at her, almost as if he was so lost in appreciative amazement that this moment was finally coming to fruition. It was blowing both of their minds before they even managed to get to copulation. Still locked in an impossible stare with him, Clara's free hand was trying to push down the fabric of his boxers. With a blink, his brain slowly registered what she was attempting to accomplish, and his hands reached down to make quick work of it.

Clara's eyes dipped down to survey her prize and the whine that simmered in her throat was completely salacious. He was taut and hard-pressed for her, still grasped beneath her fingers. She resumed her stroking, now able to make the full and complete twist of movement around him. There was a symphony of delight being emitted from above her as she felt his entire body shudder.

Regaining some sort of coherent thought, his mouth devoured her, starved and ravenous as Clara continued her ministrations. His mouth and body shifted gears, beginning their descent down her body in his mission to divest her of her lace panties. Nic's hands, fingers, and mouth worked in poetic tandem across her skin. He was taking his time testing every square inch of her torso for a reaction and what sort of sound he could elicit from her.

His fingers were already curling into the thin straps along her hip bones before his mouth was even close. The fabric scraped down the skin of her thighs and she arched her pelvis up against his chest. Her core aching against the chill but burning from within. Clara's gasp was sharp and immediate as his fingers tenderly brushed between her legs, the material in a tangle around her ankles. With a quick shift of her feet, the fabric was deposited against the bedding. She was free to part her thighs, inviting him in.

Taking the invitation without hesitation, his touch was surer with every stroke along the outside of her folds. As his mouth was paying reverence to the smooth and quivering skin of her abdomen, Clara felt a single finger slowly press inside. There was a sharp hitch of her breath as the touch was a welcomed reprieve from the beckoning heat. The gentle slide was just enough to satisfy her at the moment, but inside it stoking the fire.

Nic felt her clench around his digit and there was a heated exhale against her southern hairline as his mouth caught up with the ministrations of his hands. A second finger eased inside of her. Her moaning was lovely and high-pitched, encouraging him to brush the pad of his thumb against her bundle of nerves. The combination of touches caused Clara to arch her hips up in offering to him and it was now her turn to clutch at the bedding. His thumb moved away only to be immediately replaced by a lingering kiss which turned into a timid suckle.

The noise of utter satisfying delight was loud enough to perhaps alert his neighbors and Clara quickly bit down on her lip to suppress anything further.

"I don't care if anyone hears…it lets me know I'm doing something right." The husky tone was moist and hot between her legs as he murmured them against her most intimate area. To encourage her further, he withdrew his fingers to slide the breadth of his tongue up her entire slit with a sigh, taking great delight in how incredibly wet she was.

Clara lost herself to a mess of whimpers as he continued. There was some subtle rustling and she realized that it was the noise of a condom being unwrapped. His one hand was unfurling one down his length in short strokes while he kept her occupied between his mouth and free hand. She was on birth control but bless this man for thinking of her without even asking.

Once he was fully and safely encased, he slid the hard leanness of his body up against hers to recapture her mouth once again. Nic was still breathless from bestowing her delights and there was a subtle gleam of her desire against the dimple of his chin. Her thighs parted for him, and his hips easily slipped into the welcoming divot. The heat of his hardness was pressed against her belly, and she swallowed back her delighted anticipation.

Gazes met and there was a curl of a smile at the edge of his lips as Clara reached up to caress his face.

"All I wanted for Christmas...was you."

There was a breathy exhale of a quiet laugh from her, and his smile quickly turned into one of his wildly handsome grins. "I really want to tell you that was corny, but hell if it isn't the most romantic thing a man has ever said to me." Clara exhaled out in a breathy mess of words before pulling him in for a voracious embrace. The soft playfulness quickly burned to ash as the heat resumed between them both. Nic's palms were adjusting the opening of her thighs as he aligned himself up with her.

There was a sudden impetuosity with both of their mouths as her fingers scraped through his hair as he gingerly pressed inside. The advance was slow. He could feel her incredible tightness grasping at him. His girth held her breath hostage as she adjusted around him, fully and eagerly enveloping him inch by delicious inch. Once fully seated, he took a long moment to relish the overwhelming feeling of her as she regained a more regulated breathing pattern.

Nic parted from her lips just so he could stare into the intense abyss of Clara's eyes as he claimed her. There was a press of his forehead to her as he adjusted his grip to gradually withdraw and slide himself back into her. Her lower lip quivered as she was able to feel the unhurried drag of his manhood against her walls. He filled her so completely, simultaneously giving her body what it craved and making it yearn for so much more.

Clara's hands grasped onto him in any way possible. His resolve to keep up this languid speed was both welcomed and caused her brain to riot with the impossibly slow stoking of the fire. Nic was taking his time with her, paying homage to the temple of her body all while discovering what was going to make her crumble. Past lovers had been rather selfish in their taking of her. Sometimes Clara managed to get something out of it. But Nic was something perfectly different.

He took great care in fulfilling her, secretly wanting to see how quickly and how many times she could come undone with his attentions. Warm hands meander across her body as he thrust, giving her an all-encompassing experience that she was never going to forget. Why had she been so timid in her advances with this more than adequate lover right across the street? Right now, she was in the throes of the thought of spending the entire holiday break in one of their beds to make up for lost time.

There was a deep jolting thrust that pulled a melodic moan from Clara's parted lips. He was able to reach that impossible spot of pleasure deep within her confines with ease. Trying it again, her head arched back to the bedding, voicing her delights to the darkness. His panting mouth tried to bestow her neck with feverous kisses, but his own noises of gratification stalled his efforts. They were searing and breathy against her skin, so close to her ear for her to easily absorb them.

Clara could feel that swirling ebb and flow of searing heat gathering in her abdomen. Nic groaned, feeling her slick walls contract around him as her body hovered on the precipice of utter fulfillment. Grasping onto her, he pulled her as close as he could manage, sliding his palm along her side and around the curve of her bottom to hook her leg around his waist. With the change in angle, he was hitting her deeper still and it was only mere moments before she felt that slow swell of heat before the sparkling explosion throughout.

With a drawn-out and lingering whimpering cry, Clara orgasmed. Her hands clutched desperately at the skin of his back and his mussed auburn hair as she tumbled endlessly into oblivion. Nic wanted to watch the entirety of her in her bliss, but he was quickly becoming overcome with all of her delicious stimuli. With a surprised staccato shout, he felt his own powerful release completely overwhelm him. The second peak of her orgasm was quick and punctual, taking her breath away from the unexpected suddenness.

Nic's hips shakily stilled above her, dropping down fully against her pelvis, utterly spent. The two of them were panting heavily, bodies quiet and still reeling through the aftershocks. Clara's eyes managed to flutter open only to be met by a pair of shimmering blue eyes looking down at her expectantly. How could she convey to this complete vision of a man that she was fairly certain she left your body in heaven somewhere?

"Wow." Was the only thing they could manage to say, a mutual breathy acknowledgment of what had just occurred. It only made the both of them erupt in quiet laughter as they kissed and enveloped each other. Nic gave her a lengthy kiss before rolling over to dispose of the used condom into a tissue on his nightstand. His withdrawal caused her breath to stall, already missing his intimate warmth.

Finally noticing the cockeyed positioning of them upon his bed, Nic sat up fully to gaze down at Clara from over his shoulder with a smirk. "As much as I don't really want to move, I feel that we may need to reorient ourselves." With a questioning look, she propped herself up on her elbows and surveyed the current predicament with a laugh. The pillows had somehow ended up on the floor and the two of them had left the comforter in a rumpled mess. Although what had amused Clara most of all was the fact that she had been perilously close to the bottom corner of the bed.

"Oh...well I suppose we should." Rolling onto her stomach, she retrieved the pillow from the floor of her side of the bed only to be greeted by Nic's timidly concerned face.

"I mean...I don't want to presume that you'd stay the night..." Placing his pillow back against the headboard he turned back to her.

With a soft incredulous huff, Clara crawled up to bed to kneel next to him, cupping his jaw to press a kiss to his delighted smile. "After something like that, I wouldn't dream of being anywhere else except in your arms." Obliging her, his arms suddenly and fiercely encircled her. He grinned wildly, pulling her down onto the bed next to him. With a fierce tug, he loosened the bedding beneath them both and pulled it up over top, encompassing their intertwined bodies as Clara settled comfortably into the pillows.

"Ah well...sweet dreams it is then."

Sweet dreams indeed.

Chapter Eleven

The morning dawned, quiet and bright from the freshly fallen snow. Stirring slightly, Clara noted that she was actually warm and cozy for once, not curled up in a ball against the chill of her empty bed. Except she wasn't in her bed, and she wasn't alone. Strong arms had her in a tight grasp around her waist and her cheek was nestled against a muscular shoulder.

Murmuring her satisfied delights, Clara brushed a smiling kiss against his collarbone. That elicited a sleepy smile from Nic as fingers slowly stroked up and down the small of her back. Her eyes fluttered closed, languishing in the tender moment.

"Mmm...Merry Christmas."

"Merry Christmas, Nic." She could feel the warmth of his gaze down upon her and she tilted her chin up so she could meet his eyes. His smile grew instantly warmer, and she reached up to caress his cheek. Now succumbing to the allure of his mouth. Clara felt his hand graze against her cheek before tangling in her hair. Despite still being hazy from sleep, the kiss was wildly deep and managed to take her breath away.

Rolling towards Clara, Nic pulled her impossibly closer. His hands fanned out to mold every part of her torso against his. There was a sharp surprised gasp as she felt his rigid hardness against her thigh. Pulling away slightly he blushed and shrugged his shoulders.

"Ah…sorry. It's-uh been a while since someone shared my bed."

"Nic…" Clara looked up at him with a rather pleased smug smile. "I will never ever be disappointed waking up to…" Her hand slipped between them in a swift and fluid movement. Encircling his firm length without hesitation his breath sharply hitched to her utmost satisfaction. "…this." Grinning, her free hand stroked the side of his face before leaning back in with another kiss. "This has been the best Christmas ever. And it's only Christmas morning."

Chuckling somewhat nervously, he returned her affection as his body relaxed with her reassurance. Although with her continued motions his breaths were beginning to turn to muted noises of want. Even though the two of them had been quite satisfied the night before, there was a continuing craving that was unspoken but very apparent between them both.

"I can't help it…" Nic feigned a pout with mock innocence, gritting his teeth against her onslaught. But his voice dropped to a husky grit, deciding to tease her right back. "All I've been able to think about since our first kiss was how much I wanted to get you into bed." His words did just what he intended them to do, sending a hot wave of desire to course through her body.

Grasping a hold of his face, Clara pulled him in for a sweltering kiss. With her attention now elsewhere, his hands roamed over her body, devouring as they went while his mouth did the same. It was heated but lingering, a sustained sultry contact as his hands moved to entice her desire along further. One hand coaxed the length of her leg to wrap around his hip while the other made its way to slip between her thighs.

A satisfied groan made its way into Clara's mouth from his. His lips became more desperate with the presence of her generous slick desire against his fingers. Honestly, just looking at the man would have sent her body into overdrive. The pure fact that they were naked, in his bed, while he was aching and hard for her was already a given for her to be wildly aroused. Nic's fingers parted her folds to ease two fingers inside, easily coaxing a trembling whimper from her. There wasn't going to be much teasing needed. His free hand fumbled behind him to awkwardly open the bedside drawer and pull out another condom.

Shifting back into a more comfortable position, the kiss grew more heated. The two of them were lost in intimate contact while their bodies continued to move and coax each other further. Clara's hand scraped across his chest while her other moved between them to grab ahold of the condom stuck between his fingers. Ripping it open, she unfurled down his length and there was a hitch of his breath with her bold action. Since she had a hold of him, she began to ease him towards her craving heat. Nic answered her call, removing his fingers to grasp ahold of her hip while adjusting the positioning of her thigh so he could slip between them.

With his advance, Clara removed her hand to tangle into his wildly mussed hair. Tongues and teeth were added to the mix of their wanting kisses as she felt him ease his way inside her. There was a rough exhale against her mouth as he inserted himself with ease. Clara was so tight and grasping around him. The languid coax of his hips worked her open so he could press deeper.

Lying on their sides and facing each other, this quiet Christmas morning interlude was wildly intimate. The positioning was not for something fast and hard but something more teasing and slower. Clara could feel her body alight with each thrust and withdrawal. Forget coffee, incredible morning sex with an equally incredible man was one hell of a way to start the day. As much as she wanted to stay all day like this, her body was screaming to be pushed over the edge. She was ready to do something rash to get there.

Pushing him back onto the mattress, her lips parted roughly, and his eyes went large in delighted surprise. Straddling him quickly she sank down on him with a shuttering sigh. Fiery blue eyes coursed over the enticing view of her naked torso, his hands reaching up to caress her breasts with the tenderest of touches. With the added stimuli of the view, Nic was close. Clara watched as his face contorted and relaxed with his noises of delights. The sounds she could draw out of his man made her body feel like it was being caressed and incinerated at the same time.

It was his turn to startle her mid-thrust, as he sat up and enveloped her in his arms to press wet and breathy kisses to her neck and chest. There were grunts that accompanied them as Clara felt the sharp uptick in his hips to answer every rock of hers. Nic was the first to succumb, burying his face into the crook of her neck with his panting cries. His hot breath coursed over her heaving breasts, and she shivered from the overload to her senses.

Clara buried her fingers into the swath of his hair and arched her neck to cry out into the chill of the room feeling her orgasm overtake her all at once. Nic's arms and hands grasped her tightly, relishing in the feel of her moving against him while she chased and succumbed to her high. As her waves of euphoria waned, she slowly relaxed into the strength of his arms. He grazed delicate kisses along her collarbone as she caught her breath once again. Tenderly he cradled her and eased her back down to the mattress with him.

Clara stretched out with a completely contented sigh but grimaced slightly as she felt the wrapper of the condom against her back. Shifting, she was able to extract the offending foil packet and deposited it on the nightstand closest to her. Her eyes just so happened to catch sight of his digital clock which read 11:03 am. Laying back down with an oof from the bedding, she pressed her palm to her face with a grumble.

Currently, it was four hours past the time that Clara wanted to put the ham on to cook so that it would be ready by lunch. At this point, they'd be lucky if it would be done before dinner. Nic pulled her back into his arms, holding her in a tight bear hug for a long moment before brushing a kiss against her shoulder.

"Are you all right?"

"Yes…but-" Clara whined and turned her chin to look at him with concern on her face. "I just should have put the ham on to cook three hours ago."

Laughing, Nic kept her still tight within his grasp. "I think we will be okay if we shift things around a bit. Don't worry." With a disgruntled sigh, Clara nodded lightly, knowing he was right. Her body was still tense, and he knew that it was going to bug her if she had to sit around and think about it. "How about this? You head over and start, and I'll come over after I shower, with some lunch. You can put me to work to you help you."

It was then that her body melted against his and she lifted her gaze to look into his eyes. "That's actually a great idea." Clara kissed him fiercely with a breathless smile. "Seriously, how are you this amazing thing that's been living across the street all these months?" Nic shrugged, trying to remain nonchalant but the smile that slipped across his lips betrayed all that.

Giving him one last longing look, Clara scooted out of his bed and dressed, his cerulean eyes locked onto her graceful movements. He managed to get out of bed himself as she was buttoning up her shirt. Now it was her turn to be rather distracted as he addressed the used condom and slipped on his discarded boxers. From what she could steal quick glimpses of, his body was quite the vision and those boxer briefs were like a second skin against the enticing firm roundness of his behind.

Nic followed her out into his living room, coming up behind her to give her a kiss as she was grabbing her coat. Clara's smile was effortlessly genuine with his display of affection, and she slipped her boots on before turning to him and wrapping her arms around him.

"I'll be right over, I promise." He laid a kiss on her lips before slipping into a wicked grin. "We have to break in your house next." The pink in her cheeks was just a subtle sign of the red-hot fiery tirade that just went through her body. With a quick bite of her lower lip, she stole another kiss before slipping out his door with one last gaze at him.

Clara descended his stairs quickly, not bothering to tie her boots or zip her coat as Nic had left her rather flustered with his promises for later. The street was left unplowed with only a few tire tracks from those traveling for the holiday. She was almost skipping through the unblemished fluff when the greeting from a neighbor stopped her in her tracks.

"Merry Christmas, Clara." Called Mrs. Fitz as she meandered down her driveway to meet her. Still lost in her good mood, she smiled back warmly.

"Oh, Merry Christmas, Mrs. Fitz!" Her smile faltered slightly as she neared Clara, her eyes giving her a thorough once-over. She felt that flush returning, terrified for a moment that the neighbor could read her mind.

"Looks like you had a fun Christmas Eve." The dog sniffed at her shoes with Mrs. Fitz's tease. Clara's back went rigid in her embarrassment, and she tried to keep her face as innocent as possible.

"Oh, I-um. I had dinner with a friend."

"Is that what they're calling it nowadays?"

There was a rather vain attempt to swallow back her uncomfortableness, but her mouth had gone dry. Laughing bashfully, Clara absentmindedly tugged on the zipper of her coat. "Oh…well I-I should get Christmas dinner started. I hope you had a wonderful Christmas." Flashing a quick smile, she hurried up her driveway.

Calling after Clara, Mrs. Fitz set off down the street with her dog, "I know you sure did!"

Chapter Twelve

As Clara managed to get into the shower, she promised herself to avoid Mrs. Fitz at all costs for the near future. She had caught a glimpse of herself in the mirror in the foyer when she arrived back at the house. No wonder the neighbor had questioned her excuse. The buttons on her shirt were askew and buttoned incorrectly. Not to mention the disheveled mess of her hair that she neglected to do anything with after she had woken up. It was without a doubt that Mrs. Fitz knew what she and Nic had been up to the night before.

Grimacing with her renewed embarrassment, Clara stepped into the searing hot water with a sigh. She had set the ham in the slow cooker with a hearty drizzle of honey and brown sugar before settling on a shower. Between the two rather lengthy lovemaking sessions, she needed one before entertaining company. While washing her hair, she reminisced the events of the prior evening. Smiling to herself as she could feel that welcome heat bubbling in the depths of her belly.

The shower was quick, and she dried off with an easy French braid of her hair before wandering into the bedroom to get dressed. Clara toyed with the idea of perhaps forgoing getting dressed altogether. Of course, nothing would get done at that point…except maybe her. The rumble in her stomach dissuaded that idea for now, but it might be something the two of them could try later.

Donning her red velvet dress pants, she paired them with a silky lace camisole with a deep neckline that teasingly enhanced her cleavage. No more questions anymore on whether Nic had any sexual interest in her. That interest was now quite apparent. Clara donned a black cardigan to keep off the chill, but she was hoping that he would enjoy the ensemble.

Clara was busying herself in the kitchen when she heard the front door open, and her name being called. Closing her eyes, she relished in the moment, adoring the thought of having Nic be a regular guest in her house. After discarding his boots and coat he found her in the kitchen. She looked over her shoulder at him with a warm smile. With a lean against the wide doorway, he drank her in for a long moment, crossing his arms against his red plaid dress shirt.

"Are you ready to help?" Clara teased with a perk of her brow as he had not moved in closer to her yet.

"Sorry…just admiring the view." Sauntering over with a grin, he leaned over her shoulder and kissed her cheek. "So, what do I need to do?"

"You have the fun task of peeling potatoes." Handing him a peeler, she passed him the colander full of scrubbed potatoes.

"Got it." He nodded with a chuckle and set to his task. "This I can do."

Laughing, Clara went back to her upright mixer, already well on her way to making the dough for rolls. She had her wireless speaker playing some upbeat Christmas music and the two of them settled into their work. The silence was comfortable as the both of them were just delighted to be in one another's presence. Happy to be with each other.

Thoroughly engrossed in her kneading of the dough, Clara startled slightly when she felt warm lips against the back of her neck and hands low on her hips. The smile that slipped across her mouth was instant and she bit her bottom lip as her fingers curled deep into the heft of the dough.

"So, this is how you do it, huh?" Nic's chin was now perched on her shoulder and his eyes were watching the nimble movements of her fingers. Clara chuckled and continued on with a sprinkle of flour against the board.

"Not very exciting."

"Yeah, well if it tastes anything like everything else you've made, I'm already won over."

The two of them finished up, leaving the food to bake in the oven while the ham was close to ready. Clara had busied herself with setting the coffee table and Nic had been set with the task of getting a fire going. The setup was slightly fancier than their casual first dinner together. She was still putzing with napkins when a white box hovered just within her peripheral vision.

Glancing over her shoulder there was a question in her furrowed brow as Nic smiled coyly.

"What's that?" Clara asked as she slowly stood up to face him. He pressed closer to her, still presenting the square box with a red bow.

"Merry Christmas, Clara," Nic said softly as she gingerly took the gift into her hands. He shoved his hands into his pockets and looked on with bashful expectancy. Clara stood there, lost in her surprise but also warmed by the thought of a gift. Keeping the box grasped in her hands, she shot him a sheepish look herself before wandering over to her tree. Tucked behind the curtain was a wheeled lap desk with a large red velvet bow in a hefty bloom on the surface.

"Oh well then… Merry Christmas, Nic." Biting her lower lip, Clara wheeled it over to him and he laughed with his delighted surprise.

"You had that hidden the whole time?" Stepping closer he gave the gift a thorough once-over at all the features. "Wow… This will sure beat using my coffee or kitchen table as a desk." His eyes lifted up to hers and sparkled brightly before he grasped onto her hand to press a kiss to the back of it. "Thank you." With another kiss his eyes moved back to his forgotten gift, still clutched tightly in her other hand. "It's your turn now."

"Oh! Uh…right." Cupping the package between her hands, Clara looked over the shimmering white wrap to find an open edge. Ripping the paper, she found a lovely, lidded linen box. Letting the shreds fall to the floor, she lifted the lid and peered in. She couldn't help the burst of laughter at what was tucked inside. It was a sterling silver charm bracelet with a single charm of a bright red little car with a Christmas tree strapped to the top.

"Oh, my goodness…I can't believe you found something like this." Clara was still holding the box, lost in her surprise. Nic dipped his fingers inside the box to fish the bracelet out. His delicate touch grazed against her wrist as he clasped it on her. "A reminder of my embarrassment." Clara teased with a glance up at him, noting how close he was to her. His eyes were soft and gentle.

"It's the moment that I fell for you." The words were hushed. Clara's eyes were locked with his as she swallowed slowly. Her heart impeccably burst. One of the more embarrassing moments of her life was the one that had made Nic hers. Dropping the box on the top of the desk she swiftly wrapped her arms around his neck. She molded her body against his in one fell swoop as she captured his mouth in a wildly heated kiss. Answering her embrace, his arms enveloped her as his lips slanted against hers.

The harsh buzz of the timer went off in the kitchen and her shoulders dropped as she pouted against his mouth. "Sorry…" Clara muttered bitterly with an awkward laugh, pulling away to tend to the food. Trying to catch his breath, Nic ran his fingers through his cropped hair before following after to assist.

Dinner went off without a hitch, just four hours later than Clara's original lunch plans. She had set the coffee table up in front of the fire for the cozy ambiance as twilight started to fall. The extras from Nic's charcuterie board had been a welcomed snack in between the cooking and baking. The full Christmas meal now had them both completely content. Between the ease of the meal and the bottle of wine, the two of them had been lost in the conversation about anything and everything.

Nic was so incredibly easy to talk to. Now that there was no longer that unmentioned sexual tension between them both, there was more ease with the conversations and body language. Of course, there were also endless smiles and laughter with flirtatious touches as it was rather difficult for the two of them to keep their hands off each other for any amount of time. They both now were snuggled together on the rug, propped up against the coffee table and watching the fire.

"I took the rest of the week off," Clara murmured suddenly and Nic looked down at her with an arch of his brow. "I hadn't planned on it but the last thing I want to do is go back to work tomorrow."

Chuckling with a nod, he turned his eyes back to the fire. "I did too. Actually, I did something crazy, and I took off until after the New Year."

Knowing how difficult it was for Nic to part from his work it was her turn to look up at him with surprise. "Really? Why?"

"I wanted to spend it with you." Fiery blue eyes caught hers with a lopsided smile. "If that's okay…"

Clara's smile was warm as she lifted her hand to cup his cheek and lean against him. "Maybe I should too… You're more fun to do than work." A light blush grazed the peaks of his cheeks as he laughed.

"Well, I would hope so." He teased right back before stealing a kiss. His eyes shifted down, admiring her choice of outfit once again. "Any chance I'm going to get a closer look at this?" His fingers were already fumbling with the edge of her cardigan, sliding half of it down and over her shoulder. There was a subtle sharp inhale as his eyes flitted over her swath of skin and the thin strap of her lacy camisole.

"I think you're already well on your way…" Clara's tone was sultry as she looked up at him through hooded lashes with a cheeky smile. He couldn't help the grin, caught in the act as he was now quickly removing the sweater from her body.

"I behaved all afternoon." He reassured her, not that she was ever going to protest.

A chill went up her spine and she shivered, looking back up at him expectantly. "Now what's going to keep me warm?" Clara's taunt was low on her lips, her mouth curling around the words.

Both brows raised high up on his forehead, his heart racing from the open invitation. In the span of a blink, he enveloped her in his arms, twirling her around his torso and laying her down on the plush rug in front of the fireplace. A small noise of surprise left her mouth before it dissolved into giggles. Reaching up, she cupped his jaw. Her fingers took their time to caress and trace the features of his face while they smiled at each other.

"I thought that was rather obvious." Nic crooned as he dipped down to capture her lips. He hovered above her, propped up on flexing arms as the both of them took their time with the kiss. Strong thighs straddled the length of her, keeping her steady as the kisses grew more heated. With a subtle grin against his mouth, she reached up to curl her fingers into his belt loops and gave them a sharp tug down.

Nic faltered slightly in his stance with her aggression. With a suck of her lower lip, he dropped his body down. Clara sighed in utter satisfied delight with the weight of him molded against her. Her fingers moved to slip under the tail of his shirt, scratching against the warm skin of his lower back. There was a subtle push of his hips into her pelvis and that rush of heat hit her quickly.

Snaking her hands around to the front of his torso, her fingers began to work their way undoing the buttons of his shirt. Turnabout was fair play after all as Nic had rid her of her sweater, now she needed to rid him of his shirt. As the sides fell open, she immediately pressed her palms against the ridges of his muscles. The sheer hard feel of him under her touch would never cease to bring her that flash of utter need.

Tossing his shirt aside, he pulled his mouth from Clara's to flash her a quick grin as his mouth started its descent down her neck. He suckled and tasted the flushed skin, drinking her in with every caress. His hands had moved south, working on the fastener of her pants, and giving them a swift tug down to her knees. Kicking them off herself, his hands moved to his belt and jeans, making quick work of the removal of them before pressing back against her.

In the firelight, Clara could manage a better observation of his body as his kisses moved across the crest of her breasts and then further south. His auburn hair shimmered vibrantly with the amber glow while sculpted shoulders jutted out to either side. They rippled with movement as his hands were pushing the silk of her camisole up and over her head. There was a subtle flicker of elated awe as she decided to forgo a bra altogether.

Descending swiftly, he cupped the mounds into careful palms to lay siege to the creamy skin. His tongue twirled around a nipple with a soft suckle before pressing kisses to the base and along her sternum. Soft murmurs of appreciation warmed her skin as he continued further south, dragging his fingers down her sides to curl into the waistband of her panties. Clara's breath hitched in her throat as he cast his eyes back up to her, moving down her legs with the panties following.

A shiver ascended up her body with the display and her fingers curled into the weft of the carpet as he bared her to him. The searing look of besotted yearning stalled her breath before his hands gently eased her thighs apart. He kept those cerulean blue eyes on her as he bent down, pressing an open-mouthed kiss between her legs. Clara's back immediately arched with a throaty gasp amongst the crackle of the fire.

Nic's lips worked in delicious tandem with his tongue, tasting and teasing her open. Shuttering, she let out a mewl but bit her lip in a vain attempt to control herself.

"No need to be quiet here, darling. I want to pull every delicious noise out of you." Clara's brain had initially been hung up on the endearment but completely flatlined when his mouth suckled around her bud. The gasp he drew out of her was followed by a whimpering moan and she could feel that devilish grin between her legs.

Clara's hands shot down to tangle fingers into his auburn hair, pressing him deeper. Nic obliged without question, adding two fingers to the mix. He eased them in slowly and there was an approving groan hot against her skin. He felt her grasping and sodden around his fingers. His free hand wrapped around the front of her propped-up thigh, tugging her hard against him as he pleasured her orally.

With her mind going completely blank, Clara gasped and writhed underneath him. His fingers quickened their pace as he felt her clench around him, wildly close to her peak. Panting and whimpering her fingers tugged on his hair, quickly losing her composure as he continued his vigorous pleasure. With a harsh cry, she felt the impossible clenching deep within, sending fire radiating throughout her body as she succumbed to his ministrations.

"Oh…Nic…" Clara gasped, still rather breathless but now able to coordinate some semblance of words. He had withdrawn himself gently from her sensitive core with a soft kiss. There was a crooked grin against his shimmering lips, still glistening with her excess delights.

"Warm now?" He quipped in a murmur, nipping at her jaw as he hovered on all fours above her. Sliding her hands up his chest, Clara's eyes watched the movement before meeting his expectant gaze.

"I could be warmer…" Clara's words were sultry as a slow smile ticked at the corner of her mouth.

"Oh well…then by all means…" Bending down he captured her lips. "Let us continue." Her arms gladly wrapped around his neck and pulled him back down to her as her fingers raked through his hair. Clara could feel the rigid hardness scraping against her thigh and she wanted nothing more than to feel his entire naked self against her body.

Slipping her hands down his back, Clara eased the stretch of fabric down over his bottom, taking her time massaging and worshiping the roundness. Nibbling on his bottom lip she slid her hands around to the front to ease his manhood from its hold with care. A hot sigh hit the skin of her cheek as her fingers curled around him. His hands moved to shove down the rest of the fabric before kicking it off somewhere behind him.

The salacious sigh Clara emitted tickled his jaw as he molded his naked body to hers. The feeling was her safe place, satisfaction with the innocent intimacy. Her hands coasted across his body, admiring the subtle flex of his muscles as he lay above her. Nic's eyes were soft upon her face as he reached up to graze the pads of his fingers across her cheek.

The moment was soft and tender as they looked upon each other, skin aglow from the firelight and flushed with their earlier endeavors. Lying with him like this was almost as good as the sex. Almost.

"I don't think I've ever felt this much joy with someone before," Nic whispered to her, pressing his forehead down against hers. "Who knew that I'd be making love by the fire to an incredible woman on Christmas."

Clara flushed with his tender admission and smiled as her eyes glistened ever so slightly. "You've made what I thought was going to be a miserable holiday into one I'll never forget."

Their lips met, soft and tender with touches that followed. At that moment she wanted nothing more than for Nic to make love to her. Clara's hips rocked beneath his, pressing up and enticing him. Pulling his mouth from hers, he caught sight of her bracelet on the hand that was caressing his hair. With a soft smile, his fingers encircled her wrist, bringing it up to his lips so he could press a kiss against the chain of his gift.

It was a quick distraction for her as he turned to tug his discarded jeans closer. Clara couldn't help the grin from the tender touch as he pulled out the usual protection. Slipping her eyes downward, she watched him unfurl it along his length, admiring the gloriousness that was all of Nic. His gaze shifted back up to her flushed face and she smiled as he leaned back in for a kiss.

Coaxing her thighs up and around his waist, Clara felt him press inside and that wild fulfillment blossom throughout her body. Her arms answered in a fierce embrace around him. Arching her hips up, his breath caught in his throat with her sudden enticement. Gripping onto her hips, he answered her back with the complete and smooth sheathing of himself that caused her to whimper.

The thrust of his hips was slow but deep as she felt the scrape of his length against her slick walls. Shuttering with her delights, her ankles locked against his bottom, holding him tight to her. Nic's hands raked up her sides, absorbing her body inch by inch with his possessive touch. Rocking together, they found that intimate beck and call so effortlessly.

With one hand gripping onto Clara's waist and the other with fingers splayed out against her jaw and neck, he held her there as the power of his thrusts increased. The grunts and gasps were timed with his rhythm, and she was left breathless from the fire in his eyes as he stared down at her with intensity. Her hands grasped at every part of him that she could manage, wanting to absorb the very commanding essence that was Nic.

Clara's breath hitched suddenly with his steady increase in pace and her back arched, pressing her breasts against his chest. Seeing the desperation in her eyes he knew she was close to her climax. Bending down he kissed her, a kiss so hard and deep that it took her breath away. Breaking the kiss with a whimpering cry, she felt the rapture of her peak encompass her, tumbling off into the nether of oblivion with her noises of delight.

Holding Clara close, Nic watched her euphoria with broken moans of his own. He did his best to keep himself restrained enough to watch her fully ride out her waves of pleasure, but his release was imminent. She felt his nails dig into the skin of her hip as he snapped his against hers, giving himself over to oblivion. Burning his face into the crook of her neck, she felt his heady cries against her searing skin as he pulsed inside her.

Breathless and spent the two of them lay there, dazed, and delighted with the ending to Christmas. Clara's arms enveloped him, keeping him close as his ragged breathing slowly returned to normal. The grin on her face was unstoppable as she looked up to watch the dancing shadows on the ceiling. There was a gentle nuzzle of nose and lips against the column of her throat before he lifted his head to gaze down at her with a smile of his own.

Tender fingers caressed the stray strands of hair off her forehead and Nic adjusted his hold on her to something warmer and more delicate. Clara's legs had fallen slack to either side of him, although her thighs still cradled him between her legs. Reaching up, she caressed his cheek, pressing her thumb against that beauty mark on his right cheekbone. Tipping his chin down he peppered her with sweet soft kisses, and they shared a soft putter of laughter.

"Best Christmas ever."

Merry Christmas to all ... and to all a good night!

Printed in Great Britain
by Amazon

17090062R00052